"I Wanted To Make Love To You So Bad That Day, I Could Taste It."

Reggie tipped her face to his. "Why didn't you?"

He peered down at her. "Well...because," he finished lamely.

"Because I was the boss's sister? Because you were afraid of what Harley would do to you if he caught us?"

Cody frowned. "No, because I was three years older than you."

"Three years. Big deal."

"Yeah, it was a big deal," he replied defensively. "You were sixteen, and I was nineteen, legally a man who was supposed to know better than to play around with innocent young girls."

"I'm not sixteen anymore, Cody," she reminded him, smoothing a hand across the flat plane of his stomach. "And I'm not innocent."

Cody sucked in a breath. "No," he agreed, as the breath rattled out of him on a sigh. "You're not."

Dear Reader,

This month: strong and sexy heroes!

First, the Tallchiefs—that intriguing, legendary family—are back, and this time it's Birk Tallchief who meets his match in Cait London's MAN OF THE MONTH, *The Groom Candidate*. Birk's been pining for Lacey MacCandliss for years, but once he gets her, there's nothing but trouble of the most *romantic* kind. Don't miss this delightful story from one of Desire's most beloved writers.

Next, nobody creates a strong, sexy hero quite like Sara Orwig, and in her latest, *Babes in Arms,* she brings us Colin Whitefeather, a tough and tender man you'll never forget. And in Judith McWilliams's *Another Man's Baby* we meet Philip Lysander, a Greek tycoon who will do anything to save his family…even pretend to be a child's father.

Peggy Moreland's delightful miniseries, TROUBLE IN TEXAS, continues with *Lone Star Kind of Man*. The man in question is rugged rogue cowboy Cody Fipes. In *Big Sky Drifter*, by Doreen Owens Malek, a wild Wyoming man named Cal Winston tames a lonely woman. And in Cathie Linz's *Husband Needed,* bachelor Jack Elliott surprises himself when he offers to trade his single days for married nights.

In Silhouette Desire you'll always find the most irresistible men around! So enjoy!

Lucia Macro

Senior Editor

Please address questions and book requests to:
Silhouette Reader Service
U.S.: 3010 Walden Ave., P.O. Box 1325, Buffalo, NY 14269
Canadian: P.O. Box 609, Fort Erie, Ont. L2A 5X3

PEGGY MORELAND
LONE STAR KIND OF MAN

SILHOUETTE *Desire*®
Published by Silhouette Books
America's Publisher of Contemporary Romance

To Carolyn and Jerry Hawes. Thanks for answering
all my "dumb" questions about birthin' calves.
Your patience is equaled only by the goodness
of your hearts!

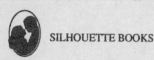

SILHOUETTE BOOKS

ISBN 0-373-76096-5

LONE STAR KIND OF MAN

Printed in U.S.A.

PEGGY MORELAND

published her first romance with Silhouette in 1989. She's a natural storyteller with a sense of humor that will tickle your fancy, and Peggy's goal is to write a story that readers will remember long after the last page is turned. Winner of the 1992 National Reader's Choice Award, and a 1994 RITA finalist, Peggy frequently appears on bestseller lists around the country. A native Texan, she and her family live in Round Rock, Texas.

Dear Reader,

There's only ever been one woman for me.... Regan Giles... my Reggie. We pretty much grew up together, our homes being less than a mile apart. When we were youngsters, she was like a kid sister to me, but then, as we grew older, my feelings for her changed to less-than-brotherly ones.

Reggie had it pretty tough growing up. She lost her father, her mother, then her stepfather. If that wasn't bad enough, her stepbrother's wife took an instant dislike to her and made Reggie's life a living hell. Since she didn't feel she could go to her stepbrother with her troubles, she turned to me for comfort. She made me feel important, needed, loved. And for a man without a family of his own, that made me feel pretty darned good.

But then everything went to hell in a hand basket. Reggie decided she couldn't take living at home anymore, and she asked me to run away with her and marry her. Though there was nothing that would've made me happier, I had to tell her no, because I had nothing to offer but a run-down cabin and the salary I earned working on her family's ranch. And I felt Reggie deserved more.

I've had years to regret that decision. Reggie ended up running away without me, telling no one of her plans or her destination... and I lost her—the only woman I've ever loved.

And now she's back in Temptation, even prettier than I remember, and a successful businesswoman to boot. She broke my heart the last time she left...and it seems she's determined to break it again when she leaves this time. But how can I ask her to give up everything she's worked for and stay in a two-bit town like Temptation, Texas, with a broken-down cowboy like me?

Prologue

Cody squinted against the darkness in the hayloft. "Regan?" he called softly.

"O-over here," came her muffled reply.

Quickly Cody climbed the last few steps and hurried to the pile of hay where she lay sobbing and dropped down to a knee at her side. "Honey, what's wrong?" he asked as he gathered her into his arms.

"She burned them," she cried, curling her fingers into fists against his chest. "She burned them all."

Cody knew without asking who "she" was. Susan Kerr, Regan's sister-in-law, her stepbrother's wife. He'd known as soon as he stepped into the barn and heard Regan's sobs coming from the hayloft above him that the two had had another fight. More often than he cared to think about, Cody had found Regan just so, crying her heart out after crossing swords with Susan.

"What did she burn?" he asked gently.

"Everything in Mother's trunk. Her pictures, her wedding gown, m-my christening dress."

All the memories of the mother she had lost. Hugging her to him, Cody felt her pain as if it were his own. "I'm sorry, Reggie. So sorry."

"Why does she hate me?" she cried helplessly, clinging to him.

"I don't know," he murmured, trying his best to soothe. When she continued to cry, he sat down on the scattered hay, pulling her to his lap.

Regan curled against the warmth of his chest, accepting his comfort as she had so many times in the past. "You're all I have, Cody," she said, her breath hitching.

Because he knew what it was like to be alone, Cody tightened his arms around her. "That's not true, sweetheart. You've got Harley."

She jerked free of his arms. "No, I don't," she cried angrily. She scrambled to her feet and crossed to stand before the hay door that opened from the loft to the outside. Moonlight limned her shape.

She stood, arms folded beneath her breasts, staring out into the darkness in silence for what seemed like an eternity to Cody. He wanted to go to her, but knew that no matter how many reassurances he offered her, she wouldn't believe him. Not when she was this upset.

He watched a sigh shudder through her. "You're all I have, Cody," she said again. The anger was gone, but her voice was still thick with tears. "And all I need." She turned then, holding out her hand to him. "Make love to me, Cody," she whispered.

Cody rose, his gaze fixed on hers, his conscience warring with his own needs. "Reggie, we can't. You don't know what you're saying. You're only seventeen. You're—"

"I'm a woman," she told him, lifting her chin defiantly. With trembling fingers she reached to free the top button on her blouse. "And I know what I want. And what I want, what I've always wanted, is you."

Cody took a step nearer, thinking to stop her. "Reggie, don't," he murmured. But she ignored him, freeing another button, then another, until her fingers all but raced down the length of her blouse. When she reached the last, she shrugged out of the shirt and tossed it to the hay.

Cody stopped, frozen by the sight of her bare breasts, full and ripe, rising and falling with each heaved breath in the shaft of moonlight coming through the hay door.

"Tell me you don't want me," she dared him, reaching for the snap of her jeans. Without waiting for an answer, she kicked off her shoes and peeled the jeans down her legs. She straightened, lifting her chin in challenge. "Tell me you don't want me as badly as I want you."

Cody swallowed hard, trying to form the words to voice the lie she demanded of him...but he couldn't. He wanted her, had wanted her for more than a year. But he was three years older, supposedly wiser, and had kept his needs in check, knowing that he had to wait until she was of age...until he had something more to offer her than what he had now.

Sensing his hesitation, Regan took a bold step, closing the distance between them. With her gaze on his, she lifted a hand to his chest. "I love you, Cody. Tell me that you love me, too."

Though he tried his damnedest to remain unaffected, the pressure of her fingers burned their way through to his heart, weakening his resolve. He closed his hand over hers, holding it against his heart. "I do love you, Reggie. You know I do, but we can't do this."

She took a step nearer, pressing her naked breasts against his chest and wrapping her arms around his neck. "Make love to me, Cody. Please," she begged.

The wall of control Cody had managed to keep between them crumbled at the feel of her body pressed against his. "Oh, Reggie," he moaned, gathering her tight against him. "We shouldn't do—"

Regan silenced his arguments by crushing her mouth over his. Boldly, she kissed him, showing him in the only way she knew how that she was more than ready to take this final step into womanhood.

Though Cody tried to keep a grip on reason, on sanity, the tender bites on his lips, the stab of her tongue into his mouth, the rake of fingernails down his back, slowly robbed him of all rational thought.

"Regan—" But before he could say more, she pulled him down with her to the hay.

They rolled, both fighting at the buttons on his shirt, the snap on his jeans, until Cody was as naked as she. Bracing himself above her, he looked down at her, his heart beating violently in his chest. Her cheeks were flushed, her eyes glazed with heat as she reached for him, drawing his face to hers.

He knew it was wrong, knew that he should do something to stop this before it was too late... But he was powerless to do anything but give in to the needs that had been escalating for months, leading to this moment. Stolen time alone, kisses that had started out innocently enough, but ended leaving them both breathless and wanting.

He'd dreamed of this, even prayed for it, but nothing had prepared him for the reality, the beauty of Regan, his Reggie, lying naked beneath him, the burning heat that raged through him at the seductive pressure of her body flattened against his.

On a ragged sigh, he claimed her mouth, teasing it open with his tongue as he guided her thighs apart with his knees. Slowly, he lowered himself over her. At the first touch of his hardened manhood, she arched away, moaning against his mouth. He withdrew slightly.

"This might hurt a bit," he warned, knowing it was her first time.

"I don't care, Cody," she whispered breathlessly. "I want you. All of you."

Easing down again, he slipped a hand between them, wanting to prepare her for what was to come. Teasing the folds apart, he dipped a finger inside. She bucked against his hand.

"Oh, Reggie," he groaned, trying desperately to hold on to the thin threads of his control.

But she wouldn't allow him that slim hold. She lifted her hips, stretching her arm to meet him and guided him inside.

At the first thrust, she gasped, sinking her nails into his back. Fearing that he'd hurt her, Cody pressed hot kisses across her face. "I'm sorry, Reggie. I didn't mean to hurt you."

"No," she murmured, wagging her head in denial. "You didn't. Please," she begged, "just—" The plea dangled uncompleted between them, for Regan, in her inexperience, didn't even know what to ask for.

"I know, sweetheart," he soothed, and began to slowly move inside her. "Just follow me."

Regan did follow him, mimicking his movements until they took on a life of their own. Passion built, dampening her skin in a fine mist of perspiration, hardening into a tight knot of frustration low in her abdomen as she raced along with him. Squeezing her eyes shut against the mist of pain/pleasure that threatened to smother her, she strained, reaching for that elusive flood of pleasure she somehow knew awaited her.

Instinctively, she wrapped her legs around his waist. "Cody," she cried. "Cody, please!"

Gathering his arms at her back, he rose to his knees, bringing her with him, and buried himself deep inside her. She arched hard against him, throwing back her head. The explosion was simultaneous, rocking them both to the very core of their souls.

Breathless, his heart pounding against the wall of his chest, Cody braced an arm at her waist and a hand on the loft floor and lowered her, following her to the hay. Rolling to his side, he gathered her close, smoothing her damp hair from her face. She lifted her head to look at him, and amber eyes softened by passion met his in the moonlight. The trust and love he saw there squeezed at his heart.

My Regan. My Reggie. The thought swelled in his chest. A man fragmented by a solitary life suddenly felt whole.

"I love you, Reggie," he whispered as he pressed his lips to her forehead.

"And I love you," she whispered in return, snuggling against him.

He held her, one hand knotted in the coal-black hair that curtained her back, while with the other he traced the curve of her waist, the gentle rise of her hips, the slope of her thigh.

Regret came then, sneaking up on him like a ghost in the night. He'd taken Reggie's virginity, robbed her of her innocence. He'd allowed lust to overrule common sense. He tightened his hold on her, knowing full well that what he'd done was wrong, but knowing, too, that if he had it all to do over again, he'd do the same thing.

Worries crowded his thoughts, one piling up on the other. What would they do now? He couldn't marry her. Not yet. She was too young and he too old. She was the boss's sister and he was nothing but a wrangler on her family's ranch.

"Cody?" she murmured.

"Hmm?" he murmured, distracted by his troubled thoughts.

"Run away with me."

Startled, Cody lifted his head to stare at her, sure that he had misunderstood. "What?"

"Run away with me. We can get married and have a place of our own. Please, Cody," she begged, sinking her fingers into his arms. "You're all I have."

Though it broke his heart to do so, carefully, Cody set her away from him. "No, Regan. I can't."

One

Silence. It pressed from every corner of Reggie Gile's private office, a constant, if not painful, reminder of the fact that she was alone. Silence really didn't bother her, nor did being alone. She'd had years to learn how to live with it peaceably. It was what the silence represented that she found so disconcerting.

Not so many months before, she might have avoided the silence and the loneliness by picking up the phone and calling her friends, Mary Claire and Leighanna, and making plans for the evening. But they were gone now, both having moved to Temptation to start their lives anew.

She almost laughed at the irony of that. Temptation. Her friends had gone there to start over, to the same town she'd run from ten years before. But of course, Mary Claire and Leighanna didn't know that.

That was Reggie's little secret…or was it Regan's? She almost laughed at the absurdity of the question. She hadn't thought of herself as Regan since she'd left Temptation. Along with her past, she'd given up her name, choosing instead to call herself Reggie, the nickname used exclusively by—

No, she wouldn't think about him now. That was another secret.

Secrets, Reggie thought on a weighty sigh. Everyone had them, but few could keep them, not like she had. She'd kept hers for ten long years, although the burden of carrying them had never seemed as oppressive as it did now. Every call from Mary Claire and Leighanna from their new home in Temptation, every mention of the town they'd moved to and the people they had met, every invitation for a visit brought with it a guilt, a yearning that weighed heavily on her heart and mind. Never had she longed for home more than she did now. Never had she wanted so desperately to give up her secret for the opportunity for a past, for a future, for even a glimpse of those she still held dear.

But she couldn't. She knew that. A person could never go back and reclaim what she had so foolishly tossed aside.

Saddened by her thoughts, she pushed away from her desk and the contracts she'd been reading and settled her spine against the soft, cushy leather of her chair. Unerringly her gaze went to the wall opposite her desk and the Georgia O'Keeffe original that hung there. Soothing in its simplicity, the painting's bold colors drew her as strongly as they had on the day she'd first seen it hanging in a gallery in Santa Fe; a radiant yellow sunflower projected on a background of cornflower blue.

She'd purchased the painting for the memories it drew of the fields that surrounded her childhood home where sunflowers had grown, tall and proud, their cheery, smiling faces tipped to the sun. The memories of home were vivid, if distant, and secreted away in her heart along with those of the loved ones she had lost—some to death, others sacrificed for a freedom that she'd once thought so important.

The phone rang, jarring her from her thoughts. Since it was after office hours, she was tempted to ignore the call and let the service pick it up, but she knew who was more than likely on the other end of the line and knew, too, that she couldn't avoid this conversation forever. On the third ring, she punched the speaker button. "Reggie Giles," she said briskly.

"Do you *ever* return calls?"

In spite of the feelings of apprehension that pricked her, Reggie found herself smiling. "Hello, Mary Claire. How are you?"

"Fine now. Hold on a second. There's someone here who wants to talk to you."

Reggie grabbed for the corners of the desk and curled her fingers around the burled wood in need of something, anything, to anchor herself to. She didn't want to talk to him. Not now when she hadn't had an opportunity to prepare herself for this confrontation.

"Reggie! We've been calling you for days! Where have you been?"

Reggie wilted at the sound of Leighanna's voice, collapsing against the chair's back, her fear giving way to relief. Another reprieve. How many more would she receive before her past caught up with her?

"Working. Where else?" she replied, trying to keep her tone light.

"Well, I'm glad we finally caught you. I have news, we both do. Mary Claire? Are you on the extension?"

"Yes, I'm here."

"Okay. On the count of three. One...two... three..."

"We're getting married!" they chimed in unison, laughing.

Reggie's eyes widened. She'd known Mary Claire and Harley were getting married, had even suffered a tremendous bout of guilt for not attending their engagement party, had already spent hours fabricating excuses for not attending the wedding. But Leighanna now, too?

"Both of you?" she asked, sure that she had misunderstood.

"Yes," Leighanna replied, laughing gaily. "Hank asked me to marry him and I said yes!"

"We've decided to have a double wedding," Mary Claire added. "And we want you to act as maid of honor for both of us. Isn't this exciting?"

Exciting? How about a nightmare? It was all Reggie could do not to put her head down on her desk and cry. She could just see Harley's face when his stepsister Regan, whom he hadn't seen since she'd run away from home ten years before, walked down the aisle toward him.

"Well, of course it is," she replied, trying to force a level of enthusiasm over the knot of dread choking her. Already mentally reviewing the list of excuses she'd offer when she declined their invitation, she asked, "When's the big event?"

"In two weeks and don't you dare say you can't come."

"It *is* short notice," she hedged.

"It wouldn't matter if the wedding was months away. You'd still find an excuse not to come. Some big real estate deal pending. A client from out of town you had to entertain. A remodeling on one of your rental properties that you had to personally oversee. We aren't accepting any excuses this time, are we, Leighanna?"

"Nope," Leighanna confirmed in a no-nonsense tone. "You're serving as our maid of honor and that's that."

"It's going to be a small wedding," Mary Claire explained, before Reggie could start offering excuses. "Weather permitting, we're having it in Harley's backyard. We've just finished remodeling the house, but a garden wedding has such an appeal. We're only inviting a few friends from Temptation and, of course, Harley's children will be there."

Tears burned behind Reggie's eyes. *Harley's children? Tommy and Jenny?* How many years had it been since she had seen them? They'd be almost grown now. Would they remember their Aunt Regan?

"You don't even have to shop for a dress," Mary Claire assured her, unaware of Reggie's state of distress. "You can wear that darling blue silk sheath with the matching jacket that you wore to the Chamber of Commerce banquet in the spring. It'll be perfect with the color theme we've chosen. And you'll adore the best man," she added. "He's a doll. I think I've mentioned him to you before. Cody Fipes? He's the sheriff of Temptation and a good friend of both Harley and Hank."

Cody? Pain, red-hot and searing, burned its way through Reggie's heart at the mention of his name and she had to press her fingers to her lips to stifle the sob that rose to her throat. She could see him still in the hayloft that night so many years ago when she had thrown herself at him, begging him to run away with her and marry her. He'd held her tight in his arms, offering her comfort as he had so many times in the past...then had broken her heart by steadfastly pushing her to arm's length and telling her that he couldn't marry her. Another year, he'd told her, and she'd be able to make the decision to leave without running, without tying herself to a man who had nothing to offer her.

There was a moment of silence while Reggie struggled to choke back the tears, the memories, the regrets.

"Please say you'll come, Reggie," Leighanna begged. "It would mean so much to me. To both of us."

Reggie gulped back tears, knowing that if she ever gave in to the emotion she might never stop crying. Her heart warred with the secret she'd harbored for so long and the longing to be a part of her friends' wedding and their lives. If she agreed, her secret would be out and she would have to face them all. Harley, Tommy, Jenny...Cody. If she refused, she would disappoint Mary Claire and Leighanna, and ultimately lose two friends whom she held dear.

"I can't," she finally managed to choke out. "I'm sorry, but I just can't."

The road to Temptation stretched before Reggie like a ribbon of silver in the bright sunshine. She drove with her hands cinched tight around the steering wheel of her Lexus, praying with each passing mile that her arrival wouldn't ruin what should otherwise be the happiest day in her friends' lives.

The decision to attend the wedding hadn't been an easy one, in fact she'd vacillated almost daily. She'd carefully weighed the pros and cons, just as she did every decision she made. The pros were obvious: continued friendship with two dear friends and, she hoped, the renewal of a family relationship she'd turned her back on ten years before. The cons were just as obvious and a whole lot more daunting: having Harley call her Regan and expose her secret, subjecting herself to possible rejection and public humiliation, seeing again the man who had rejected her, the man she'd never been able to forget.

In the end, cowardice had given way to duty and love and she'd decided to take her chances, telling no one of her plans, hoping that the element of surprise would work in her favor.

As she drove through Temptation, she kept her gaze focused on the road ahead, denying herself even a glance at Carter's Mercantile, Will Miller's barbershop or any of the other landmarks that remained from her childhood. There would be time enough for a nostalgic tour later, she promised herself. But for now she had to reach Harley's ranch where the weddings were to take place.

She had timed her arrival carefully, waiting until the very last minute to appear, hoping to avoid seeing anyone other than Leighanna and Mary Claire before the actual wedding took place. With her hands damp on the wheel of her car, she turned onto the drive, parked behind the other cars and trucks already there and climbed out, pausing only long enough to listen.

The murmur of voices and soft strains of music came from the backyard, and she knew, as she'd prayed, that everyone was already gathered there, waiting for the ceremony to begin. With her heart pounding in her chest, she hurried to the front door. Taking a deep breath, she stepped across the threshold of her childhood home.

Once inside, she closed her eyes, fighting back the ghosts that rushed at her, then opened them to look at the room where her family had once known such happy times...before tragedy had struck, robbing her of her mother and stepfather, before Harley had brought home his bride, Susan.

She steeled herself against the hate that flooded her. She wouldn't think about Susan now. Wouldn't think of the cruel things she'd said and done. She wouldn't think of how miserable Susan had made her life, until Reggie had finally run just to escape the torment.

She was here for a wedding, she reminded herself. A celebration of life and love. She wouldn't think about the past. Only the present.

Certain that the brides would be in the master bedroom, waiting to make their entrance, she slipped down the hall. She found them, just as she'd expected,

in the room once shared by her mother and stepfather.
The sight of the two of them brought tears to her eyes.

Wearing an ivory suit, Mary Claire sat in front of
a cheval mirror. Leighanna, dressed in soft pale blue,
stood behind her, struggling to pin Mary Claire's veil
into place.

"For heaven's sake, Mary Claire!" Leighanna
fussed. "Be still or I'll never get this on straight."

"I *am* sitting still," Mary Claire snapped impa-
tiently. "It's your fault the dang thing's crooked.
Your hands are shaking like a leaf."

In spite of her own nerves, Reggie bit back a smile.
"Here, let me," she offered from the doorway. "After all, that is one of the duties of the maid of honor,
isn't it?"

Both women whirled, mouths gaped wide at the
sound of Reggie's voice.

"Reggie!" they both cried and bolted for her.

The three met in the middle of the room, gathering
each other in a tearful hug. Mary Claire was the first
to pull away. "I knew you would come! I just knew
it!"

Leighanna sniffed, dabbing at tears with one hand,
but refusing to let go of Reggie with the other. "She's
lying," she said, casting a disdainful look Mary
Claire's way. "She's been crying for hours, cursing
you because you refused to come."

Mary Claire's chin came up. "Oh, and what were
you doing?"

"The same," Leighanna replied without batting an
eye. "But at least I'm not too proud to admit it."

"Girls, girls," Reggie admonished, laughing.
"This is no time for squabbling. This is your wedding

day!'' Giving Leighanna's hand a squeeze, she took the pins from her, then guided Mary Claire back to the chair. ''Now let's get this veil in place before y'all start pulling out each other's hair and there's nothing left to anchor it to.''

At that moment, the door flew open and Mary Claire's daughter Stephie burst into the room, her crown of spring flowers slightly askew. ''Mama, hurry up! The preacher said it's time.'' She stopped short when she saw Reggie.

''Reggie!'' she squealed and threw herself at Reggie, wrapping her arms around her waist. ''You came!''

Laughing, Reggie dropped down to her knees, giving Stephie a quick hug before leaning back to straighten her headpiece. ''Yes, I'm here. I wouldn't have missed this—'' she glanced at her two friends behind her and laughed. ''Rather, *these* weddings for the world.''

Stephie twirled for Reggie's benefit, showing off her new dress. ''I'm the flower girl and Jimmy's the ring bearer. He's a 'fraidy-cat and refused to walk down the aisle, so he gets to stand by the preacher.''

Remembering the purpose of her errand, she grabbed Reggie's hand, tugging her to her feet. ''Come on! We have to hurry! The preacher said it's time.''

Reggie slowly rose, turning her gaze on her two friends. Drawing a deep fortifying breath she reached for their hands. She squeezed, knowing she had to prepare them in some way for what was about to take place, but not at all sure what to say.

''You're the best friends a woman could ever ask

for and I wish you both all the happiness in the world." She swallowed and blinked back the tears that clogged her throat, thinking about what was to come. "No matter what happens today," she said, her voice growing hoarse, "please know that I love you both like family."

Before Mary Claire or Leighanna could respond to the odd comment, Reggie took Stephie's hand and let the child lead her from the room.

Reggie stood behind the screen of ivy that concealed the kitchen doorway from the guests, her hands resting on Stephie's shoulders, listening with Stephie for the music cue from the harpist. Hearing it, she stooped to press a kiss on the top of the little girl's head.

"Remember," she whispered. "Walk slowly and don't forget to drop the rose petals."

Stephie tipped up her chin, grinning at Reggie. "Don't worry," she whispered back. "I won't forget. I've been practicing all morning."

Reggie watched the child step into the center of the arbor and turn, selecting a petal from the basket she carried. With a wink at Reggie she dropped it then moved out of sight.

Reggie pressed a hand to her stomach, knowing that on the other side of the screen of ivy, at the end of the stretch of red carpet, her stepbrother, Harley, waited. What would he do when he saw her? she wondered frantically. Would he cause a scene? Would he demand an explanation for the ten years of silence? Would he even recognize her after so many years?

And Cody? What would be his reaction? What would be *hers* on seeing him again?

Before her fears could carry her further, the screen door opened behind her and Mary Claire and Leighanna stepped out onto the narrow porch, both looking radiant. Mary Claire quickly thrust a single, long-stemmed rose into Reggie's hand and nodded as the music cue sounded for her entrance. With a last wistful look at her two friends, Reggie stepped into the center of the arbor and turned to face those gathered.

She paused on that spot of carpet, flanked by an arbor of green ivy and baskets filled with a rainbow of roses, carnations and baby's breath, her fingers clutching tightly at the single rose she held. Her gaze settled instantly on Harley. Dressed in a suit, his hands folded properly in front of him, he was handsome, achingly so, and the mirror image of his father, the stepfather Reggie had loved so dearly.

Oh, Harley, she cried silently. *Please don't be angry with me for doing this.*

At that moment, his gaze met hers and for a second there was no change in his expression, then slowly, ever so slowly, recognition dawned. His eyes widened, his shoulders stiffened...her name formed wordlessly on his lips. Blinking back tears, she took that first slow step toward him, then the next, her heart crying out for his acceptance, for his forgiveness.

When she reached him, she stopped, daring to rise to her toes to brush a kiss on his cheek. "Please don't be angry," she whispered at his ear. "I've come home."

His hands closed at her elbows, painfully so, cut-

ting like steel vises into her tender flesh. For a moment, she thought he meant to rebuke her, to cast her
away, as she had her family ten years before. But then
his grip eased. She felt the tremble in his fingers as
he released her, and she lifted her face to his. She
nearly wept when she saw the tears that glistened in
his eyes. He raised a hand and brushed it tenderly at
her cheek as if to assure himself that it was not a
ghost standing before him.

"Regan," he murmured, his voice a hoarse whis-
per.

"Later," she promised softly. "We'll talk later."

At his slight nod, she turned away to take her place
on the opposite side of the minister. When she turned
back, the music swelled and she shifted her gaze to
the arbor just as Mary Claire stepped beneath the
arch.

She watched, emotion tightening her chest, as her
friend and soon to be sister-in-law started that slow,
life-changing walk down the carpet, unaware of the
drama that had just taken place. Once Mary Claire
had laced her arm through Harley's, Leighanna followed, her gaze never once wavering from the man
who stood at Harley's right.

Reggie shifted her gaze to look at him. Hank Bra-
den. She didn't know him, at least not personally, but
like everyone else who'd ever lived in Temptation,
she knew him by reputation. *You better be good to
her,* she warned silently as Leighanna took her place
at his side.

The harpist ran her fingers across the strings, then
pressed them, silencing the harp as the minister

opened his Bible. "Dearly beloved," he began. "We are gathered here..."

Then, and only then, did Reggie find the courage to look farther, to the man who stood at Harley and Hank's right.

Cody.

Her heart stuttered to a stop at the sight of him, then kicked into a rib-rattling beat. Like the two friends he stood up for, he was breathtakingly handsome, dressed in a dark western-cut suit and crisp white shirt, his hair freshly trimmed and slick against his head. She'd forgotten how handsome he looked in a suit, for the memories she had locked away in her heart were steeped in jeans and boots, a cowboy hat that changed with the seasons and a warm, lazy smile that had always had the power to both arouse and comfort her.

At the innocent age of seventeen, she'd thought him grown, mature...a man. As she looked at him, she realized how childish, how foolish her assessment had been, for it was a man who stood before her now. His shoulders had broadened over the years, his chest had filled out, and even from beneath the camouflage of his suit she could see the increased strength in his muscled arms and legs.

He'd changed so much...and yet so little. Now, like then, she found herself wanting to lean against that strength, to let those muscled arms envelop her as they had so many times in the past, offering comfort and protection from a life that seemed out of her control.

But Cody seemed unaware of her need. His attention focused on the minister, he listened intently as the vows were exchanged. With all her heart, Reggie willed him to look at her, to let those lips firmed in concentration spread into a welcoming smile directed her way.

But he didn't. He kept his gaze on the minister, never once glancing her way.

"You may kiss your brides."

At the minister's invitation, both Harley and Hank gathered their brides into their arms and kissed them with a fervor that had the guests cheering. Their faces wreathed in smiles, the two couples linked arms and made their way back down the strip of red carpet.

Reggie knew what came next. She'd served as bridesmaid in enough weddings to know the script by heart. She shifted her gaze back to Cody and found him looking at her. Her breath caught in her lungs as gray eyes met hers. She didn't know what she had expected from him. A sign of welcome, maybe. A yearning for what might have been. Perhaps even a little regret. But never this cool disregard.

He offered her his arm, but she could tell that he did so only out of obligation to his duties as best man.

She tipped up her chin, refusing to give in to the tears that threatened, and slipped her hand through the crook of his arm. Heat flooded her body with an awareness of his nearness as he silently walked her down the strip of carpet. Their hips brushed once. Twice. And Reggie's heart crowded her throat.

She wouldn't cry, she told herself. Not now. There'd be plenty of time for crying later.

Cody looked around the kitchen. The wedding guests were gone. Tommy and Jenny had left to make the drive back to their mother's home in San Antonio. Stephie and Jimmy were knee-deep in a video game in Jimmy's newly redecorated bedroom. All who remained to celebrate were the newlyweds, Cody...and Regan.

He wanted to kick himself into next month for not paying more attention to the wedding plans when they were discussed. But when the women had started talking colors and flowers, he'd tuned out. Now it was too late to prepare himself for the shock of seeing Regan again. She was here and ready or not, he had to deal with both her and the memories she'd left with him.

Arms folded across his chest, his hip resting against the newly tiled kitchen countertop, Cody felt separate from the group huddled around the table, talking. An outsider. It seemed he'd always been on the outside, looking in.

He'd all but grown up with Harley and Regan. His family, if you could call them that, had lived less than a mile from the Kerrs' ranch. With no one at home but an alcoholic father, Cody had spent most of his time at the Kerrs', preferring their company to that of a drunk. The Kerrs had welcomed him to their home and hearts, a gesture Cody would be eternally grateful for, but he'd always been careful to remind himself that he wasn't truly a member of the family, merely an outsider who had gained entry out of pity.

Even so, he'd grieved with them when Harley's mother had passed away. Celebrated when Harley's father had brought a new wife and stepdaughter to live with them. He'd accepted big-brother responsibilities for Regan right along with Harley and tried

his best to honor them even when his feelings for
Regan changed to less than brotherly ones.

He'd grieved again when Regan's mother had died.
He'd even served as a pallbearer when Harley's father
had been killed in a freak farm accident less than a
year after his second wife's death.

But the pain of those losses paled in comparison
with the pain he felt now. Regan. She was home. But
for how long?

Though he didn't belong there, didn't feel he had
the right to sit in on what should be a private family
reunion, he couldn't bring himself to leave, not when
there were so many questions to be answered, questions he didn't have the guts, or the right, to ask.
Instead, he stood on the sidelines and listened while
the answers unfolded before him.

"I thought you would come for me and drag me
home by my hair," Regan was saying as she shot a
teasing glance at her stepbrother.

Harley chuckled. "The thought did cross my
mind." He shook his head, remembering, his smile
turning wistful. "But I knew I had to let you go. By
law, you were old enough to be out on your own.
Besides, you were unhappy here. Forcing you to come
back would have only made things worse." He
sighed, reaching to gather Regan's hand in his larger
one. "I'm sorry I didn't make it easier for you here.
I was so damn busy trying to make this ranch pay
that I was blind to how bad things were between you
and Susan."

He squeezed her hand. "After I discovered what
you'd done, my biggest concern was for your safety.
When I found out that you had gone to the bank and

withdrawn all the money your mother had left you, I knew that at least you wouldn't be living on the streets." He lifted his gaze from their joined hands, his eyes filled with the love and the pride that she remembered. "You were always headstrong, independent. I never doubted that you could take care of yourself, but damn, I missed you."

Regan's eyes misted. "And I missed you. You'll never know how much."

Harley squeezed her hand again. "And now my little sister is all grown up." He studied her, his gaze growing thoughtful. "When Mary Claire mentioned her friend Reggie, I never put the two together. Giles, isn't it? Reggie Giles?"

At her nod, his forehead wrinkled. "Did you change your name to keep me from finding you?"

Reggie felt heat creep into her cheeks and she stole a glance at Cody, wondering what he'd think when he heard that she'd married. But he didn't seem interested in the conversation taking place. He seemed more fascinated with something on the tips of his boots. "Reggie just seemed to fit and Giles was my married name," she murmured.

Harley glanced around as if expecting to find a husband lurking somewhere in the kitchen. "Where is he?" he asked, returning his gaze to hers.

"Living in Spring, Texas, with his new wife and baby."

Cody's head snapped up at that. *Divorced? Regan was divorced?* Unlike Harley, he'd known Regan had married. More than a year after she'd left Temptation, he'd decided to hell with Harley and his willingness to just let Regan go without putting up a fight. He'd traced her to Houston and discovered from the court records that she'd married. Though he'd made the trip to try to persuade her to come home with him, he'd left without ever contacting her.

"You're divorced?" Harley asked in surprise.

"Yes. Our marriage lasted less than a year," she explained. "It was a mistake." She could have told Harley the mistake had been hers, that she'd married Kevin Giles for all the wrong reasons, the biggest of which was her hope of forgetting Cody. "But we're still friends," she added.

Still friends? Cody felt a stab of anger. She'd maintained a relationship with her ex-husband, but not with him. He guessed that pretty much summed up her feelings for him.

Mary Claire slowly shook her head, still dazed by all that had transpired. "After all these years of friendship, I can't believe I never knew you were Harley's sister."

"Stepsister," Regan clarified, smiling at Harley.

Harley reared back in his chair, his chest swelling in brotherly pride. "Step or full, you're still our little sister." He cocked his head over his shoulder to peer at Cody. "Right, Cody?"

Cody stiffened. The feelings he had for Regan hadn't been brotherly since she'd turned sixteen, and at the moment, even those were dampened by a blinding anger he couldn't have explained if he'd tried. One thing he knew, though—he didn't like hearing others call her by his special name. "Yeah, right," he mumbled.

Leighanna dabbed at wet eyes. "This is all so—so, heartwarming."

Hank rolled his eyes. "Here we go again," he mumbled, pulling out an already damp handkerchief.

With an indignant sniff, Leighanna snatched the cloth from his hand. "I can cry if I want. After all, it isn't every day a person gets to witness a reunion like this."

Hank snorted. "You obviously don't watch much TV. Stuff like this happens on 'Oprah' all the time. Father reunited with daughter he's never seen. Twins reunited after being separated at birth twenty years before." His eyes took on a teasing glint as he glanced at Cody. "Maybe we should call up Oprah, huh, Cody? Milk this for all its worth. It would give you another chance to sing the praises of Temptation on national television and maybe draw a few more folks our way."

Cody's face reddened at Hank's reference to all the media attention Temptation had received after Cody had suggested at a town meeting a few months back that they should advertise for women to move to Temptation to save their dying town. "Back off, Hank," he muttered.

Hank chuckled good-naturedly as he looped an arm around Leighanna's shoulders and pulled her to him for a hug. "Just a thought."

Mary Claire let out a long sigh. "Well, it just proves that life is certainly stranger than fiction."

"It does for a fact." Harley pushed away from the table. "I think this calls for a toast." He quickly filled flutes with the champagne left from the reception and passed them around. Positioning himself behind Regan, he placed a hand on her shoulder and lifted his glass. "To Regan, my sister, whose homecoming is the best wedding present I could ever ask for."

Regan's eyes widened and she bolted from her chair, setting her glass aside. "Oh! I almost forgot!" She ran into the den and returned, digging through her purse. She pulled out two envelopes and placed one in Leighanna's hand and the other in Mary Claire's. "Congratulations!" she exclaimed then folded her arms triumphantly at her breasts. "The honeymoon is on me."

Mary Claire's mouth dropped open. "A honeymoon?"

"Yes. A honeymoon. You're all scheduled to leave in the morning for Cozumel. The reservations can be changed, of course, but, hey! Why not go now?"

Mary Claire lifted her head from the tickets she'd pulled from the envelope. "Oh, Reggie, as much as I appreciate the gesture, we can't. The kids—"

"The kids," Reggie interrupted, "have their Aunt Reggie to baby-sit them while their Mom and Dad are soaking up the sun on the Caribbean."

She turned to Hank and Leighanna. "What about you guys? Anything that stands in the way of your enjoying a honeymoon?"

Leighanna started to reply, but Hank quickly snatched the envelope from her hand. "Heck no! Thanks, Reggie."

Leighanna jerked her head around to stare at him in open-mouthed surprise. "But what about the End of the Road? Who'll run the bar?"

Hank pressed a kiss on the tip of her nose. "We'll close it. It'll still be there when we get back. I'm not passing up the chance of spending a week alone with my wife.''

Though her opinion of Hank had been guarded at first, Reggie decided she might just like this guy after all. Any man who'd drop everything to spend a week with his new wife had her undying respect. She shot him a wink. "Well, that settles it, then. In the morning you guys are off for a week in Cozumel.''

Harley turned to Cody, his forehead knitted in a worried frown. "Would you be willing to keep an eye on my place while I'm gone?''

Without tasting the champagne, Cody set his glass aside. When he'd heard Regan offer to stay and baby-sit Stephie and Jimmy, he'd immediately started planning a vacation of his own. The destination didn't matter, just as long as he was far away from Temptation and Regan. But now he was trapped. He couldn't deny his friends this opportunity for a honeymoon, and, without his help, he knew Harley would never agree to go.

"You know I will," he assured Harley, as he reached for his hat. He settled it one-handed onto his head, knowing he had to get out before this madness consumed him. "I guess I better be going." He made a quick circle around the table, clasping first Harley's hand, then Hank's, offering his congratulations. A peck on the cheek for Mary Claire and another for Leighanna. But when he reached Regan, he took an obvious step back and merely tipped his hat...and then he was gone, the door slamming shut behind him.

Reggie stared after him, feeling the bitter sting of his rejection. *Why?* she wondered in confusion. Why was Cody treating her so coolly? They'd once been so close.

Well, she'd watched him leave before without an explanation, she told herself, but this time she wasn't going to let him get away so easily.

"Excuse me," she murmured to the others and rose to her feet.

By the time she pushed through the back door, Cody's long stride had carried him halfway to his truck.

"Cody!" she called. "Wait!"

He turned, but the look of repressed fury on his face stopped Reggie cold. Less than six feet separated them, but it gaped like a mile.

Reggie hauled in a steadying breath. "Is—is something wrong?"

"What do you mean?" he growled.

"You seem…" She shook her head in confusion. "I don't know…angry or something. I'd hoped that—"

He took a step nearer, his eyes darkening to a stormy gray. "What did you hope, Regan? That I'd kill the fatted calf? That I'd welcome the prodigal sister home with open arms like Harley?" He took another step nearer and the heat of his anger all but smothered her. "Well, I'm not Harley, Regan," he ground out. "And I'm not your brother. I never was and I never will be. I—" He clamped his lips together before he could say more, before he could say something he would regret.

With a scowl he turned his back on her, and headed for his truck, leaving her standing on the drive behind him.

Two

Telephone poles and road signs flashed by in a blur as Cody raced his truck through the night, venting his anger with a little speed. When the highway narrowed to two lanes he slowed to the legal limit, then stopped altogether when the pavement ended, giving way to the rock road that led to Jack Barlow's place.

He sat a moment, his arms draped loosely over the steering wheel, staring but seeing nothing. He drew a long breath. The anger was gone, or at least most of it. He could deal with what was left.

With a glance to his right, he saw the familiar gap in the fencing, the faded path of a dirt road now choked with weeds. Years before he'd stood in that gap many a morning, rain or shine, waiting for a school bus to take him to school. At the end of that dirt road, protected by darkness, lay his old home place. On impulse, or maybe because it seemed a fitting end to the day, Cody turned and headed down the road.

Ignoring the scrape of mesquite trees against the sides of his truck and the occasional *thunk* of a rock to his underpinning, Cody bounced his way down the deeply rutted road. When the cabin came into sight, he yanked the steering wheel hard to the left, then braked to a fast, dust-churning stop in front of the shadowed structure, aiming the beam of his truck's headlights dead on.

In front of him sat his inheritance, the only thing Buster Fipes, the town drunk, had left behind when his liver had finally said "No more."

Cutting the engine, Cody swung down from the truck, leaving the headlights on for illumination. At the intrusion, a trio of rats darted through a gap low on the front door and leaped from the sagging front porch, disappearing into the tangle of vines and weeds that had taken over the yard.

Ignoring them, Cody peeled off his suit jacket and tossed it onto the seat, then cuffed his shirtsleeves to the elbow as he walked to the front of his truck. He settled his back against its warm hood, then folded his arms across his chest and crossed his legs at the ankles as he stared at the place he'd once called home.

He snorted in disgust. *Home*. This place had never been home to him, or anyone else for that matter. It was merely the place where, long ago, he'd stored his belongings and rested his head on occasion. Now, it had lain vacant for more then eleven years.

At one time the property had been owned by the

Kerrs, and the old cabin used by hunters who leased seasonal hunting rights on Kerr land. But then Cody's dad had come along and cut a deal with Harley's father, promising work in exchange for ownership of the cabin and the five acres of land that surrounded it. His old man hadn't lived long enough to uphold his end of the bargain, and it was Cody who had worked for the Kerrs to repay the debt.

Cody shook his head, remembering. Harley's father had tried to talk the then sixteen-year-old Cody into simply letting him deed the land over to him after Buster had died, but Cody's pride wouldn't let him accept the gift. Instead, he'd worked part-time during the school year and full-time during the summers, then after graduation he'd hired on full-time, working on the Kerr ranch until the debt had been paid.

He'd lived alone in the cabin until he left Temptation. He'd packed up and headed out of town, seeking his fortune with the only skill the good Lord had seen fit to bless him with...riding bulls. And when he'd returned four years ago and accepted the job as sheriff, he'd chosen to live in the quarters at his office rather than try to make the cabin livable again.

When trespassers had shot out the glass panes, he'd simply boarded up the windows and tacked a No Trespassing sign on the door.... But it hadn't kept the vandals out. Not that there was anything of value inside to worry about. There never had been, not even when his old man was alive. The shack wasn't worth the price of the match it would take to burn it down.

But the place was his, he told himself. That and the five acres it stood on. Not a lot, but then Cody had never had much.

Frustrated by his thoughts, he pushed away from the truck and strode toward the one-bedroom cabin. He'd come back to the place only once after that first year of riding the circuit, then left again when he'd found Regan had gone.

Regan. The anger he thought he'd burned up on the highway came singing back with a vengeance. With a growl, he scooped an empty whiskey bottle from the weeds at his feet and hurled it hard and fast at the cabin's front door. It hit the metal No Trespassing sign and shattered, the splinters of glass gleaming like a starburst in the silver glow of the headlights.

If only he'd had something to offer her when she'd asked him to run away with her, to marry her, he thought angrily. Maybe things would have turned out differently. But all he'd had was this sorry excuse for a cabin and the wages he made working on her family's ranch. Not much to offer a woman who was accustomed to more.

So, he'd told her, no, to be patient. Another year and she could make the decision to leave home without tying herself to a man who had nothing to offer her. What he hadn't told her was that he'd be back to claim her once he had a stake.

He'd left Temptation, chasing his fortune on the back of a bull, hoping to make it big and bring home his winnings. Enough to earn him her brother's blessing when Cody asked for Regan's hand. Enough for the two of them to buy a place of their own.

But Regan hadn't been patient…or maybe she simply hadn't cared enough to wait, he thought grimly. A year after he left, soon as she'd turned eighteen, she'd hightailed it for the big city, then married some guy she'd known less than six months.

Cody braced a hand against a splintered post and dipped his forehead in the crook of his arm, wiping the perspiration that beaded his brow before lifting his head to stare at the tumbling-down cabin.

He didn't know why he'd come here. He rarely set foot on the place. He supposed he'd needed to remind himself of his roots, of the fact that he wasn't good enough for Regan Kerr—or Reggie Giles, as she called herself now. *Reggie.* Anger burned through him as he remembered the name she'd assumed upon leaving Temptation. Why had she chosen to be called by *his* special name for her? He shook his head, refusing to consider what that might mean. He hadn't been good enough for her eleven years ago, and nothing had changed much since then...at least not for him.

But he'd seen that Lexus out front of Harley's house and had known without even asking that it was Regan's. He'd listened in silence as she told Harley about the real estate business she owned, about the properties she'd invested in. If anything, the gap between them had widened over the years, not narrowed.

And now she was back.

Firming his lips against the emotion that burned through him, Cody forced himself to take slow, even breaths. He tipped back his head, his gaze on the stars overhead, searching for an answer to the question he couldn't even voice.

How would he survive when he was forced to stand by and watch her leave again?

With a vicious growl, he kicked at the rotted post, then spun and headed for his truck. Climbing behind the wheel, he turned the key and looked up, his gaze hitting on the reminder of where he came from, who he was…at all that separated him from Regan. Narrowing an eye at the cabin, he shifted into first and let out the clutch.

The truck bucked across the uneven ground, the cabin growing larger as he drew near. But Cody never once wavered from his goal. He slowed, then stopped when the bumper of his truck met the porch post. Easing off the brake, he hauled in a deep breath and stomped the accelerator to the floor.

Rocks spun behind the truck's wide rear wheels and the old wood groaned and creaked at the pressure. Cody set his jaw, feeling through the steering wheel the vibration of the post's resistance before it finally gave way with a loud *crack*. He quickly shifted and reversed before the porch roof collapsed, then he stopped again once he'd reached safety, watching as the dust settled around it.

His lips thinned in determination, he backed again, reset, aiming straight for the side of the house. Wood splintered, tin flew, dust spewed. Cody quickly reversed again and floored the accelerator, shooting out of danger's way. The wall hung at an odd angle a moment, teetering like Cody's old man had when he'd come home drunk, then slowly toppled, taking the roof along with it.

Cody worked methodically, circling his truck around the perimeter of the cabin, taking down each wall in turn, until nothing remained of the old cabin but a pile of rotten lumber and rusted tin.

Sweating from the exertion and breathing hard, he draped his arms along the top of the steering wheel, watching as the debris shifted, then settled over his childhood home. There'd been no happy memories there, so the tears that stung his throat weren't for what was...but rather for what might have been.

What did you hope, Regan? That I'd kill the fatted calf? That I'd welcome the prodigal sister home with open arms, like Harley?

Cody dropped his head to press his forehead against the back of his hands as the spiteful words he'd thrown at Regan came back to haunt him. He hadn't meant to hurt her, not when all he'd wanted to do was hold her in his arms and never let her go. But the anger of her leaving, of not waiting for him, repressed for so many years, had spewed out of him before he could stop himself.

He could still see the look of shock on her face, the hurt. The realization that he had put it there shamed him more than any words of recrimination she might have hurled at him.

He sank back against the seat with a frustrated sigh. He knew there wasn't a chance for them. There hadn't been eleven years ago, and there certainly wasn't now. And that was what had made him angry. That was what had made him turn on her, taking his frustrations out on her. It was that feeling of utter helplessness, knowing there was nothing he could do to change the way things were...and wishing like hell he had the power, the right, to claim her as his own.

But they'd been friends once, he reminded himself as he continued to stare at the pile of debris. Maybe they could be friends again…if he hadn't already ruined his chances for that, too.

He sighed, wishing with all his heart that he could have more with Regan. But he realized that friendship with her was better than nothing, and Cody Fipes had lived with nothing for too many years.

Reggie managed to hold back the tears until she was alone in her room, the same room she'd occupied as a young girl. Now, as then, her pillow absorbed her tears of frustration, of hurt, and muffled the sounds of her sobbing from the others in the house.

She tried to get a grip on her emotions by reminding herself how much she had to be thankful for. Harley had accepted her openly with no sign of anger or resentment for the past. Mary Claire and Leighanna had forgiven her for the little white lies she'd told them, for the evasions that had been necessary to protect her secret from them. Before leaving for their mother's home in San Antonio, Tommy and Jenny had even promised to visit her in Houston, and in addition to them she now had a new niece and nephew, Stephie and Jimmy, to lavish her love on.

But no matter how hard she tried, she couldn't make the hurt, the disappointment go away.

She tightened her fingers on the pillow, pressing it closer to her face to muffle the new wave of sobs that rose.

Why? she cried silently. *Why had Cody treated her so cruelly? What had she done to deserve such anger, such fury?*

She hadn't known what to expect from him when he saw her again, but nothing could have prepared her for the wrenching her heart had undergone when he'd turned his back on her and walked away.

She had carried his memory and her love for him for so many years—even through a brief marriage—clung to them through bouts of loneliness when she'd yearned for home. It was foolish to think he had done the same.

And Reggie Giles was anything but a fool.

She'd given up on tears as a solution to a problem ten years ago when she'd left home. Since then she'd learned to meet her difficulties head-on, seeking resolution through wisdom and sheer grit.

She sniffed, pulling her face from the pillow to drag a hand beneath her nose. She twisted around to a sitting position, pulling the pillow across her lap. She sniffed again, then hauled in a deep, shuddering breath.

She could do this, she told herself firmly. She could stay in Temptation for the week she had promised, then she was going back to Houston where she belonged.

And this time she'd forget Cody Fipes.

Reggie gave Mary Claire a nudge towards the car. "Don't worry about a thing. Stephie and Jimmy and I will be fine. You just concentrate on enjoying your honeymoon."

Mary Claire caught her lower lip between her teeth. "But I know how you feel about taking off from work."

Reggie lifted her face to the heavens. "This, coming from the woman who has chastised me for years because I refused to take a vacation." She dropped her gaze to Mary Claire's. "Well, I'm taking one," she said firmly. "And if I choose to take it baby-sitting my new niece and nephew, so be it. Now scoot," she ordered, giving Mary Claire another nudge. "Or you'll miss your plane."

Harley held the door for Mary Claire, then turned to Reggie. "Thanks, sis. I owe you one."

Reggie waved away his thanks. "Pooh. What are sisters for?"

Harley walked with her to the driver's side of the car. "I stored a bunch of your stuff up in the attic. If you have a chance, you might want to go through it."

Touched that he would have kept her things all these years, Reggie gave him a quick hug. "Thanks, Harley. I will."

Harley stopped at the car's door. "Cody's prom-ised to drop in every day to check on the cattle, but if you need anything in the between time, give him a call. His number's posted on the pad by the phone."

Though she stiffened at the mention of Cody's name, Reggie kept her smile in place. "I'm sure we'll be fine. Right, kids?" she asked, pulling Stephie and Jimmy to her side.

"Right," they echoed, tipping up their faces to smile at her.

Mary Claire leaned across the seat. "Now y'all be good for Reggie and mind what she says."

"We will, Mama," they promised.

Harley climbed behind the wheel and started the car's engine, closing the door behind him.

With Stephie and Jimmy at her side, Reggie waved as the car backed down the long drive; she was already plotting ways to be absent when Cody dropped by to make his check on the cattle.

Later that morning, Reggie and her two young charges were standing in the barn. "Well, of course I can ride a horse," Reggie huffed. "I grew up on this ranch, remember?"

Stephie and Jimmy eyed her doubtfully, but then Jimmy gave his shoulder a lift. "If you say so." He handed her a halter. "You can ride Mama's horse, Cupid."

Reggie wrinkled her nose. "Cupid? What a silly name for a horse."

Jimmy sighed his agreement. "Yeah, I know. But Harley named her that because he used her to play Cupid so he could talk Mama into marrying him. Pretty gross, huh?"

Laughing, Reggie ruffled his hair. "Yeah, that's pretty gross." She looked at the line of stalls. "Which one is she?"

Stephie lifted a finger and pointed. "The last stall on the right."

Reggie looked at the horse, then back at her two charges. "Okay, so do you two know how to saddle up?"

"Yep," Stephie replied proudly. "Harley said if we're gonna have horses we have to learn to take care of them all by ourselves."

Reggie remembered him saying the same thing to her when she'd received her first horse at about their age. She prayed she hadn't forgotten those hard-learned lessons.

"Well," she said, eyeing Cupid dubiously. "Let's get going then."

While Stephie and Jimmy saddled their horses, Reagan did the same…or at least she tried to. Brushing and combing presented no problems, and though she struggled a bit cleaning out Cupid's hooves, she accomplished the task. That only left saddling.

The blanket went on easily enough, but every time Reggie tried to lift the saddle to heave it onto Cupid's back, the horse sidestepped and Reggie would stagger, the weight of the saddle pulling her almost double.

With a huff of frustration, she hitched the saddle higher and lifted it again.

"Do you need any help?"

Reggie turned to find Jimmy and Stephie both waiting, holding their saddled horses by their reins. Frowning at Jimmy's offer, she turned back to the horse. "No, I'll get it this time." Setting her jaw, she lifted the saddle breast-high and heaved. When Cupid sidestepped again, she lunged, following her, and successfully landed the saddle on the horse's back. "There!" she said proudly, dusting off her hands. "I did it."

At the spatter of applause behind her, she turned. Cody stood in the door to the barn. The sun was behind him, shadowing his face, but she knew it was Cody. He'd stood, just so, a million times in the past, dressed much as he was now—jeans, boots, a cowboy hat pulled low over his eyes. For a second she was seventeen again and her heart tilted at the sight of him.

Cody saw the look of expectancy light her eyes,

the half smile of welcome curve at her lips before she could stop it, and remembered how she used to look at him that same way when he would come in after working out on the ranch all day. When he was a young man, that look had had the power to bring him to his knees. He discovered that as a man, his reaction was much the same.

Friends, he reminded himself sternly when he felt that familiar tug. *Just friends.*

"Nice job," he murmured as he stepped inside. "Need any help?"

Reggie gave herself a shake and quickly turned away, cursing herself for not having saddled the horse faster and avoided seeing him. "Thanks, but I can handle it."

Knowing he was probably watching her every move, waiting to ridicule her ineptness, she felt all thumbs as she lifted the fender and hooked the stirrup over the horn. Stooping, she reached beneath the mare and caught the girth, pulling it up and threading the leather cinch through it. Anxious to escape Cody, she quickly unhooked the halter and replaced it with a bridle, then led the mare out of the stall.

"Here," Stephie said, and thrust a pair of spurs at her. "Mama always wears these when she rides."

Reggie accepted the spurs, forcing a smile to her lips for the child's benefit. "Thanks, Steph."

Holding the reins with one hand, she bent over and buckled the spurs around the heels of her borrowed boots. Rising, she gave her two charges a wave. "Lead the way."

Cody stepped aside as Stephie and Jimmy led their horses out of the barn, but he fell in step beside Regan when she passed by him. He'd spent a sleepless night thinking about how roughly he'd treated her. Now, he hoped to clear the air a bit and maybe reestablish the friendship they'd once known. "Regan, about last night—"

She lifted her chin, keeping her gaze locked tight on the barn door. "It was a lovely wedding, wasn't it?" she replied, purposely misunderstanding him. "Mary Claire and Leighanna made beautiful brides."

Cody heaved a breath. She wasn't going to make this easy for him, but then again, nothing had ever been easy with Regan. "Yeah, they did." He scuffed along beside her, trying to find the right words. "I'd like to apologize for what I said to you. I—"

She turned her back on Cody, cutting him off, and draped the reins across Cupid's neck. "No apology necessary. I think you made your feelings quite clear." Gathering the reins at the horn, she angled her head just far enough to look at him, her eyes as cold as chips of ice. "But let's understand one thing, Cody. I never wanted you as my brother. Not then and certainly not now."

With that she stuck her boot in the stirrup and swung her leg over the saddle. But in her haste to get away from Cody, she forgot about the spurs she'd put on. When her right leg hit Cupid's side, the spur's wheel dug into the horse's flank and the horse took off, bucking, with Reggie half on, half off the saddle. Before she knew what happened, she found herself sitting on the ground with dust billowing around her.

Cody was beside her before she drew the first shocked breath. "You all right?" he asked, hunkering down beside her.

The look in his eyes registered genuine concern, but Reggie's pride was too bruised for her to notice. As far as exits went, this wasn't her most brilliant one. She gave his chest an impatient shove. "Yes, I'm all right," she grumbled as she struggled to her feet.

The horse stood not ten feet away, looking at Reggie with the biggest, blackest, most innocent eyes, as if to say, "What happened to you?"

Scowling, Reggie limped to the horse and stooped to gather the reins.

"Are we still going riding, Aunt Reggie?" Stephie asked uncertainly.

Reggie straightened, forcing a game smile though she was sure she'd be sporting a bruise on her backside the next day. "Of course we are."

In the time it took her to remount, Cody had Harley's horse and was leading him out of the barn. Fearing he planned to ride along with them, Reggie quickly headed Cupid for the pasture. "Come on, kids," she called over her shoulder. "Let's get going."

Stephie and Jimmy fell in beside her, obviously relieved that they weren't going to miss out on the promised ride. They laughed and teased as they rode alongside her, sharing with Reggie their own experiences of getting thrown.

Within minutes Reggie heard the sound of hoofbeats coming from behind and turned in her saddle to see Cody loping toward them. Groaning inwardly, she watched him rein the big horse in beside them.

"Mind if I ride along?"

Frowning, Reggie lifted a shoulder and turned

away. "Suit yourself." With a squeeze of her legs against Cupid's sides, she urged the horse into a trot. Stephie and Jimmy fell in beside her, leaving Cody to bring up the rear.

Reggie soon settled in with the rhythm of the horse's gait and relaxed somewhat when Cody kept his horse a safe distance behind her. He did gate duty, squirreling down from his horse, unlocking the gates that separated the pastures, then locking them back after everyone had passed through. Though acutely aware of his every move, Reggie never once glanced his way.

Stephie and Jimmy chattered away, pointing out this landmark, then that, whooping occasionally when a jackrabbit, startled by the approach of the horses, shot from a clump of brush and bounded through the tall grass ahead of them. Cody drifted away from the group from time to time, working his way through the grazing cattle, checking for problems; then he would silently rejoin them.

After nearly fifteen minutes of riding, they reached the north pasture where a new herd of cows milled about, some grazing lazily, others dozing beneath the shade of a stand of live oaks, swishing their tails at flies.

As they made their way through the herd, Cody gradually took over the lead. He reined to a quick stop, holding up his hand.

Reggie looked around, trying to figure out why he'd halted so abruptly. "What?" she asked irritably.

He pointed ahead to where vultures circled low in the sky. "Something's dead or dying." He kept his gaze on the birds' slow movements. "There's a ravine up ahead. I'll check it out. Keep the kids here."

Unused to taking orders from anyone, least of all Cody, Reggie frowned at his back. "You guys stay here," she instructed the children. "I'm going with Cody." She kicked her horse into a trot, following him.

Cody stopped suddenly, standing in his stirrups to listen. Reggie reined in beside him. A cow's low bawling drifted to them across the tall grass. Exchanging a worried look, they kicked their horses into a lope, quickly covering the ground that stretched between them and the ravine.

At its precipice, they stopped and looked down. A cow lay on the ground below them, her swollen sides heaving, her eyes wild as she lifted her head to look at the two humans who stared down at her.

"What's wrong with her?" Reggie asked in growing alarm.

"Looks like she's trying to have a calf."

Reggie glanced at Cody. "I thought cows calved in the spring?"

"This one must've forgotten to look at the calendar," Cody muttered dryly. He swung down from his horse and passed Reggie his reins. "I'm going down for a closer look."

While she watched from above, Cody half walked, half slid down the steep embankment and into the ravine. Once he hit the bottom, he kept his steps slow and easy as he approached the cow. He hunkered down about ten feet away. One look and he knew she was in trouble. He could see the tips of the tiny hooves already protruding beneath the cow's tail and could tell without drawing any closer that the calf was coming breech. If left to her own devices, he knew both the cow and her calf would die.

With a sigh, Cody pushed to his feet. Shading his hand over his eyes, he looked up at Regan.

Seeing the grimness of his expression, she called down to him, "What's wrong?"

"Calf's breech. I'm gonna have to pull him."

Reggie swallowed hard, shifting her gaze from Cody's to stare at the suffering cow. She'd seen a calf pulled before and really wasn't sure she was wanted to see it again. "Do you want me to help?"

In spite of the direness of the situation, Cody snorted a laugh at the reluctance in her voice. She'd always had a weak stomach when it came to watching a cow give birth. "No. What I need is Harley's truck. He's got a pull in the back, plus his vet bag." He shifted, cutting his eyes back to the cow before lifting his gaze again to her. "Would you mind taking the kids to the house and bringing the truck back here? I'll stay with the cow and see what I can do in the meantime to help her."

Reggie was already turning away, leading Cody's horse beside her. "Don't worry," she assured him. "I'll be back as quick as I can."

She put her fingers to her lips and whistled shrilly. "Hey, kids!"

Involved in a wild game of horseback-style tag, they reined in their horses and looked at Reggie.

"Want to race back to the house?" she challenged. Before they could respond, she kicked her horse into a lope and headed back the way they had come, leading Cody's horse beside her.

Three

Cody pressed a hand at the cow's neck, monitoring her pulse. It was growing weaker by the minute. If he didn't get the calf out, and soon, he knew he was going to lose the mother. He glanced at his watch. Ten minutes had passed since Regan left to fetch the truck. It would take at least another fifteen for her to make the return trip.

Tipping his face to the sun, he squinted up at the sky and saw that the vultures still circled, waiting for what they obviously considered a sure meal.

"Not if I can help it," he muttered.

He stripped off his shirt, then wrapped it around his hands for protection from the calf's sharp hooves. Murmuring encouragement and comfort to the cow, he sat down on the ground behind her. Bracing a boot on either side of her, he took the calf's hooves in his hands and waited for the cow's next contraction. When it came, he pulled, working with it.

Sweat beaded on his forehead as he strained. The muscles in his arms corded and began to burn. He dug his heels deeper into the hard-packed ground, searching for purchase, and pulled even harder, until the veins on his neck stood out in relief.

But the calf remained stubbornly inside.

Releasing his hold when the contraction ended, he drew up his knees and draped his wrists across them, breathing hard. After a moment, he dipped his forehead to his shoulder and wiped the sweat from his eyes.

From above, he heard the sound of an engine and scrambled to his feet, knowing it was Regan, returning. He quickly scaled the steep slope and saw Harley's truck bumping across the pasture toward him.

Regan braked to a stop, jumped out, then paled when she saw the streaks of blood on Cody's arms. She glanced up, her eyes filled with dread. "Is she—?" She gulped, unable to finish the question.

"She's still alive," Cody assured her. "I was just trying to pull the calf out on my own." He reached into the back of the truck and grabbed the pulls. "Where are the kids?"

"I left them at the barn, unsaddling the horses. I told them to go to the house as soon as they were finished and wait there."

He nodded his head in approval. "Good idea." He shifted the pull to his opposite hand and retrieved the vet bag. "Stay here," he ordered as he headed for the ravine. "This could get ugly."

Reggie caught her lower lip between her teeth as

she watched Cody slide over the ravine's edge, tempted this time to do as he directed. She'd watched her share of animal births and knew that "ugly" didn't even come close to describing a normal birth, much less a complicated one. But she also knew that two sets of hands were better than one when a calf needed to be pulled. Besides, this was Harley's cow, and she felt an obligation to do all that she could to help save it.

"No," she called after Cody, as she slipped and slid her way after him. "I'll help."

Cody glanced up at her, surprised by her offer, but then gave his head a brisk nod. "Let's get to it, then."

Together they slid the rest of the way down the embankment. Cody quickly went to work, strapping the brace at the cow's hips and stretching out the pull. After padding the calf's hooves with his shirt, he wrapped the chain around them then attached it to the pull.

With a glance at Reggie, he slowly pumped the lever attached to the brace, taking the chain's slack. "You might try to talk to her, soothe her."

Her hands shaking uncontrollably, Reggie moved to the cow's head and dropped to her knees beside her. That she could get that close was a testament to the cow's weakness. "It's okay, mama," she murmured, laying a hand on the cow's side. "We're going to help you bring your baby into the world."

The sun beat down unmercifully on Reggie's back, and a thin line of perspiration drizzled its way down her spine as she waited with Cody for the next contraction. An awareness of his nearness pricked at her every nerve.

She'd sat at the same distance from other men, she reminded herself firmly in an attempt to get control of her emotions, and never once suffered such a state of distress. Granted, it was the width of a conference table rather than a cow's broad back that usually separated her from them, but the difference in setting didn't explain her sudden shortness of breath, the sting of nerves beneath her skin.

She'd always found it stimulating to pit herself against her male opponents as they battled their way through the terms of a complicated real estate deal, while each sought the upper hand. But those confrontations were nothing compared to this. There was something powerful, almost primal, about watching Cody do battle with nature. His face was set in grim determination, his eyes narrowed as he waited, his body tense with expectancy.

She wanted to hate him for what he'd said to her, the way he'd treated her the night before...or at the very least hold on to her anger. But the emotions that ran through her had nothing to do with hate or anger, bordering instead on lust.

When the next contraction came, Cody put his muscle behind the lever, taking up slack, working with the cow's own efforts to deliver her calf while unknowingly drawing Reggie's gaze to his arms.

Mesmerized, Reggie could do nothing but stare. Muscles bunched down the length of his arms, while perspiration beaded on his chest. It ran in tiny rivulets through the coarse hair that matted his chest, racing down the flat plane of his stomach to darken the waist of his jeans with sweat. It was all Reggie could do to breathe.

She'd loved Cody as a teenage girl, lusted after him even then. But those feelings were nothing compared to the heat that burned through her body now. She knew it was insane, even absurd. This wasn't the time or the place to be thinking such carnal thoughts, but no matter how hard she tried, she couldn't make herself look away, nor could she banish the thoughts from her mind.

"His hips are in position," Cody called out, his breathing ragged. "Put your hands on her sides and push."

Guiltily, Reggie tore her gaze from Cody's chest and shifted, placing her palms on the cow's swollen sides. Putting all her weight on her hands, she pushed for all she was worth.

"Here he comes," he called. "Another good tug and we've got him."

Setting her jaw, Reggie pushed again, her arms quivering at the strain. From the corner of her eye, she watched the calf's trunk appear, then its head. Finally, his front hooves slipped free and Reggie fell back on her heels, grabbing for breath. Cody quickly freed the chain from the calf's rear legs, then grabbed his shirt and started cleaning the mucus from the calf's nose and mouth.

"Come on, little guy," he urged, pumping his hands against the calf's ribs. "Breathe."

Her own breath locked tight in her throat, Reggie watched him work on the calf, while she searched for a sign of life, anything to let her know this calf would live. A leg twitched, then twitched again before arcing out and giving Cody's knee a sound kick.

With a sigh of relief, Reggie dropped her chin to

her chest, offering a silent prayer of thanks before shifting her gaze to the mother. The cow lay as still as death at Reggie's side.

Fear knotted in her chest. "Is she—?" She stopped, swallowing hard to keep the tears that threatened at bay.

Cody stood, his lips pressed in a thin line of frustration as he glanced at the cow. He'd seen it happen probably a hundred times over the years, but the sense of failure never lessened. "Yeah," he mumbled as he tossed the ruined shirt to the ground in disgust. "We'll need to take the calf up to the barn."

Reggie slowly rose, unable to tear her gaze from the cow's awful stillness. "What will you do with her?"

Cody bit back a groan at the quiver he heard in her voice, then silently cursed himself for allowing her to stay. He knew how softhearted Regan was, and knew, too, that he should've never let her witness this, knowing how slim his chances were of saving both the cow and the calf.

"I'll bring the front-end loader down here and dig her a grave." Unable to look at Regan's grief-stricken face, he turned away, wrapped the calf in his discarded shirt, then retraced his steps up the embankment to lay the calf in the back of the truck. Once he'd deposited it in the back, he grabbed the cooler from the bed of the truck, poured water over his hands, arms and chest, then briskly rubbed, washing away all signs of the birth. When he returned to the ravine minutes later, Regan stood just as he'd left her, staring down at the dead cow.

His chest tightened at the sight. "Regan," he murmured, moving to stand behind her. When she didn't respond, he cupped his hands at her shoulders, intending to draw her away. "Come on, let's get you out of here."

With a strangled sob, she spun, burying her face against his chest. Surprised, Cody slowly closed his arms around her. His heart nearly broke at the anguished sound of her crying. "Shh," he soothed, moving his hands up and down her back. "We did all we could."

But the tears continued, dampening his chest as she clung to him. Cody wrapped his arms tighter around her. He held her, just as he had so many times in the past, offering comfort and a shoulder to cry on.

But with the offer came a pain so strong that it threatened to rip him in two.

He closed his eyes, willing himself to remain unaffected, but the feel of her body pressed against his tore through him, reminding him of another time he'd held her, just so. Now, like then, he found himself responding to the feel of her body pressed so tightly against his, shattering every bit of control he'd managed to hold on to. Unable to resist the temptation, he buried his lips against her hair, drinking in the pure womanly scent of her.

But even that wasn't enough to satisfy his thirst for her.

Knowing he had to separate himself from her before he did something he'd regret, he drew back a fraction and framed her cheeks in his hands. He tipped her face up to his. "Regan, I—"

But whatever words he'd been about to say died on his lips as her gaze met his. Misted with tears, her eyes were ravaged by grief but held a look of such complete trust, of such need, that Cody felt himself falling victim to their pull.

On a ragged groan, he dragged her into his arms again and crushed his mouth to hers. He felt her stiffen, and knew he should let her go...but then her lips softened beneath his. Slowly, muscle by muscle, her body relaxed and she lifted her arms to curl them around his neck. Cody had to lock his knees to keep from dragging her to the ground.

The years fell away, and they were teenagers again, giving in to temptation, sneaking a kiss in the barn when no was around to see, experimenting with the sexual tension that seemed to always hum between them. They explored and tasted, just as they had in their youth, but with the added experience that the years in between had given them.

The sun beat down on them, adding heat to a fire that was quickly burning out of control...and Cody knew he had to stop while he still had the strength, the resolve.

Reluctantly, he softened the kiss, then withdrew altogether, stroking the pads of his thumbs beneath her eyes. Their gazes met and held. He dropped his hands to her shoulders to steady them both as the ground beneath his feet seemed to shift.

Seconds seemed an eternity as they stared, each lost in the gaze of the other. Questions neither had the nerve to voice, hung between them, holding them in place.

Why did you leave me, Cody?

Why didn't you wait for me, Regan?

Why didn't you come back for me, Cody?

How could you marry someone else, Regan, when you said you loved me?

She nervously wet her lips. "I—I guess we'd better go," she murmured, dropping her gaze.

Cody hauled in a shaky breath. He knew she was right. They had the calf to care for and the children were waiting back at the house for their return. "Yeah," he replied, releasing his breath on a shuddery sigh. "I guess we had."

He dropped his hands to his sides and turned away, silently cursing himself for thinking that he and Regan could ever be something as innocent as friends.

Reggie pressed her fingers to her lips, savoring the textures and taste of Cody's kiss, wondering how it had all happened. She hadn't planned to throw herself into his arms, but when he'd touched her, when she'd felt the strength and comfort of his hands on her shoulders, she hadn't been able to do anything else. She'd needed him, just as she always had, to lean on. To share the grief and the frustration, knowing instinctively that somehow Cody would make it all right.

But then, when his lips had touched hers, she'd been swamped with a whole new set of emotions, the strongest of which were memories of another time when he'd kissed her. The last time. She shuddered, remembering. It was the same night that she'd lost her virginity to him.

Sighing, she folded her arms along the top rail of the stall and rested her chin on her hands as she stared at the orphaned calf Cody had placed there. No matter what the future held for her and Cody, she wouldn't regret that morning's kiss, she told herself, just as she'd never regretted their last time together eleven years before.

"Aunt Reggie?"

"Hmmm?" Reggie murmured, clinging to the sensations that still warmed her.

"How will we feed him?" Stephie asked.

Reggie sighed again, pushing back the thoughts of Cody to focus on the task at hand. "We'll have to bottle-feed him."

"We've got milk in the refrigerator at the house. Do you want me to get some?"

Reggie dipped her head to look at Stephie. At the earnestness in the child's expression, she smiled softly. "No, I'm afraid that won't work." She leaned to ruffle Stephie's hair, understanding her need to do something. "Come on. Let's see what we can find in the lab room to feed him."

Stephie jumped from the stall gate to follow. "But the milk in the refrigerator is cow's milk, isn't it? The same as a mama cow feeds her babies?"

Reggie bit back a smile. "Not quite, honey. By the time we purchase it at the grocery store, it's processed and homogenized. A baby calf needs special ingredients that are only found in raw milk that he gets straight from his mama." She stepped into the lab and had to stop as a sense of déjà vu rushed over her.

The room was just as she remembered it. Clean, neat and orderly. A refrigerator hummed against the far wall. A stainless steel sink gleamed on another. On either side were shelves stacked high with all kinds of supplies needed on a working ranch.

How many times had she stepped through this

door, she wondered, lugging a stray cat or dog in her arms, begging her stepfather to set a leg or stitch up a wound? No matter how busy, he'd always dropped what he was doing and offered what skills he had. Sometimes he was able to save the animals she brought to him, other times he failed. But he'd always tried, just as Cody had tried today to save that cow and her calf.

Cody again.

Reggie pushed the thoughts of him away and crossed to the shelves to sift through the items stored there, looking for a container of calf starter. She felt Stephie ease up against her side. Sensing the child's need to help, she pointed to the cabinet beside the sink. "Look under there and see if you can find a bucket with a long nipple on it."

Obviously pleased to have a job, Stephie skipped off, returning within seconds with the required bucket. Reggie accepted it absently, already scanning the side of the box. "Okay," she murmured as she read. "We're going to need a measuring cup and water."

Stephie ducked beneath the sink and pulled out a large glass measuring cup. While Stephie held it steady, Reggie filled it with the powder from the box, then gestured for Stephie to dump it into the bucket. After adding water, she stirred until the powder had dissolved. Between them, they lugged the bucket back to the stall.

Easing open the door, Reggie slipped inside, closing it after Stephie.

Murmuring softly to the wobbly-legged calf, Reggie knelt in front of it. "Here you go, baby," she encouraged, wetting the nipple with some of the sticky yellow liquid. The calf nudged at the nipple, then backed away, shaking his head as if to say "Yuck."

Stephie clamped her hand over her mouth to stifle a giggle. "I don't think he likes it," she whispered.

Reggie wrinkled her nose. "Who could blame him? It stinks something awful." But she knew she had to get the calf to nurse.

Scooting closer, she stuck her fingers in the liquid, then held them out. The calf stretched out his neck and sniffed, then took a cautious lick. Within seconds, he'd sucked Reggie's fingers into his mouth.

Startled, it was all Reggie could do to keep from yanking her hand back when his rough tongue pulled hungrily at her fingers.

"He thinks you're his mama," Stephie whispered from behind her.

A knot rose to Reggie's throat when the calf released her fingers and looked at her, bawling miserably. She quickly dipped her fingers back into the bucket and rubbed them around the nipple, then offered it to the calf again.

He sniffed, licked, then latched onto the nipple, sucking noisily. Reggie's shoulders drooped in relief.

"How's he doing?"

Reggie turned her head to find Cody standing on the opposite side of the stall wall, his arms braced along its top. His hat was pushed back on his head, his hair damp with sweat.

Their eyes met and held, both remembering what had occurred between them little more than an hour before. Reggie's cheeks burned as her heart kicked into a rapid beat.

"Fine," she replied, trying to keep the tremble from her voice. "He's taking to the bucket without much problem."

"Good."

"Did you—?"

Cody straightened, shoving the hat even farther back on his head. "Yeah. Everything's taken care of."

Reggie couldn't help noticing the fatigue in the gesture, the level of weariness in his reply. "Where's Jimmy?" she asked.

"He's out in the pasture throwing sticks for the dogs to chase."

She stood, passing the almost-empty bucket to Stephie. "Here, Stephie. Why don't you finish feeding the calf?"

Her eyes bright with excitement, Stephie settled her hands over the handle. After making sure her niece had everything under control, Reggie crossed to the stall door, opened it and stepped through.

"Oh, Cody," she murmured in sympathy as she swept her gaze down his length. "You're a mess."

He glanced down and grimaced at the smears of dust and sweat on his chest and the grime clinging to his jeans. "I guess I am." He swept a hand ineffectually across the thigh of his jeans but only succeeded in stirring up a small cloud of dust at his knees. "I guess I better head for town and get cleaned up."

Panic seized Reggie at the thought of him leaving. She didn't want him to go. Not yet. Not when it seemed they'd made a small step in chipping away at the wall that stood between them.

"Shower here," she suggested quickly, then forced

herself to take a deep calming breath. "I—I'm certain we can find something in Harley's closet for you to put on while I wash your clothes."

Cody's head came up, his gaze meeting hers. "Are you sure?"

Sure? Reggie wasn't at all sure that inviting him to stay was a good idea, and even less sure of what was happening between them. But the thought of him leaving was something she didn't want to consider. "Positive. Besides," she added, forcing a teasing smile to her lips. "Mary Claire would shoot me if I allowed you to leave without feeding you, especially after all that you've done for them today."

Cody grinned, knowing she was right, at least about the part concerning Mary Claire.

Reggie listened to the shower run as she dug through Harley's closet looking for something for Cody to wear. A shirt wasn't a problem. She simply grabbed one of the many denim shirts folded on a shelf. The jeans though...now, that was a problem. Harley was heavier than Cody by a good twenty pounds and taller by at least three inches. She held out a pair of jeans to inspect them, then groaned at the size of the waist. Grabbing a belt, she added it to the gathered items. *He'll just have to make do,* she told herself.

As she stepped from the closet she heard the shower shut off. She stopped a moment, the clothes pressed to her breasts. She could imagine him, his body slick with water, his hair mussed and dripping as he stepped from the shower. Closing her eyes, she pictured him plucking the fluffy towel she'd set out for him and rubbing it briskly over his body. Down his chest, across the smooth, flat plane of his stomach. Stooping while he ran the towel down each muscled leg. Holding a corner of the towel in one hand while tossing it across his back then catching the opposite corner behind him. Sawing back and forth across that broad expanse of manly flesh.

A sigh shuddered through her as the image grew, and she hugged the clothes tighter to her breasts.

Reggie, she warned herself. *That kind of thinking is going to get you in trouble.* Giving herself a firm shake, she headed for the bed to deposit the clothes before Cody finished in the bathroom and caught her there.

But before she could make good her escape, the bathroom door opened. Reggie spun, then froze when Cody stepped into the doorway, the towel knotted loosely as his waist. Her heart stopped, then plunged into a thundering beat at the sight of so much bare maleness. The clothes she held slipped from her grasp when her gaze settled on the towel at his waist.

Cody shifted from one bare foot to the other. "Sorry," he murmured self-consciously. "I didn't know you were in here."

Reggie tore her gaze from that strip of white to meet his gaze. Heat burned in her cheeks at being caught staring. "I—I was just laying out some of Harley's clothes for you." She stooped to gather the clothes from the floor. "There's a shirt and jeans," she said as she dumped the pile of clothes on the bed, "but you'll probably need the belt to keep the pants up. If you need anything else—" She turned, the rest of the offer dying on her lips when she saw Cody still in the doorway, watching her.

Cody wondered if she realized how beautiful she looked, standing there, her heat-glazed eyes wide and filled with uncertainty, her hair still mussed from the wind. Straw from the bed she'd made for the calf still clung to her jeans and shirt. He could see the play of nerves in the fingers that she quickly laced together, could hear it in the huskiness of her voice. But that was okay, because he was suffering a pretty strong case of nerves himself.

The kiss in the pasture hadn't come close to satisfying his need for her. If anything, it had only intensified it. He took a step toward her and she took an immediate step in retreat. He frowned, wondering if he'd misread the look of desire he thought he'd seen in her eyes only moments before.

"Can I get you anything else?" Reggie asked, her voice sounding raw even to her own ears.

"Just one thing," Cody murmured as he took another step nearer.

Reggie forced herself to remain in place, refusing to give in to the desire to run, or worse, to throw herself into his arms. Nervously, she wet her lips. "What?"

Holding her in place with nothing but the strength of his gaze, he laid a finger against her lips, tracing the path her tongue had made only seconds before. Heat infused her body as his face dipped down, then settled into a tight ball of longing in her abdomen when his lips met hers. On a sigh, she melted against him, wrapping her arms around his waist.

"Aunt Reggie!"

They jumped apart at the sound of Stephie's voice, Reggie's panicked gaze locking with Cody's as the sound of the kitchen door slamming echoed through the house.

"I'm coming, Stephie!" Reggie shouted, then whirled for the door. Cody caught her arm, spinning her back into his arms. The look in his eyes burned its way through Reggie's flesh.

"Later," he promised, dipping his head over hers again.

The kiss was way too quick but laced with enough heat to send Reggie's head spinning. Lightheaded, she stepped from his embrace, her gaze riveted on his. With a slight nod of agreement, she turned again for the door.

"Wash your hands, Jimmy."

Already halfway to the kitchen table, Jimmy stopped, slowly turning to frown at Reggie. "I just did."

"That was *before* you played with the dogs. Wash them again."

Muttering under his breath, Jimmy headed for the sink.

Suppressing a smile, Reggie picked up the tray of sandwiches she'd just thrown together and set them on the table.

Stephie beamed a smile from her chair. "Can I eat? I already washed my hands."

Reggie laughed, leaning to ruffle the child's hair. "No, we have to wait on our guest."

"Guest?"

Reggie glanced up to see Cody standing in the

doorway, his hair still damp from his shower, his hands planted on his hips.

"Since when did I slip to guest status at the Kerr table?" he asked as he crossed to Reggie's side and hooked an arm loosely at her waist.

The naturalness in the gesture set Reggie's heart racing. "Y-you're not," she stammered, her mouth suddenly dry as she remembered that "later" he'd promised. "It was just an expression, reminding Stephie of her manners."

"Just checking." Cody leaned over the table and snagged a triangle of sandwich. With a wink at Stephie, he popped it into his mouth.

Frowning, Reggie slapped at his hand. "I see *your* manners haven't improved any."

Stephie clapped her fingers over her lips to stifle a giggle and Jimmy rolled his eyes as he slumped down in a chair.

Cody shrugged and dropped into a chair, pulling Reggie down to the one beside him. "Just hungry, is all. How about you guys?" he asked, as he pushed the platter of sandwiches toward the kids. "Didn't y'all work up a pretty big appetite today?"

Jimmy greedily grabbed a fistful of sandwiches and dropped them to his plate. "You bet," he replied, recognizing a kindred spirit when he saw one. "I'm so hungry, I could eat a horse."

Reggie snagged the plate when he reached for it again, arching a warning brow his way. "Thankfully, we are having tuna sandwiches for lunch, which I'm sure the horses in the barn will be grateful for."

Obviously deciding it wasn't wise to push his luck, Jimmy picked up one of the triangles from his plate and took a wolfish bite. "So, what are we going to do after lunch?" he asked over a mouthful of sandwich.

Reggie and Cody looked at each other, both thinking about that "later."

Stifling a sigh, Cody picked up a sandwich, suspecting that that "later" might be a while coming. "I don't know, Jimmy. What'd you have in mind?"

Four

"**I** thought I'd find you here."

Startled, Reggie glanced up to find Cody standing in the stall's open door, one shoulder braced against the gate. She smiled softly, dropping her gaze to the sleeping calf she held in her lap as she resumed her petting. "I was afraid he might be lonely."

"Where are the kids?"

"Asleep. They were exhausted after all the day's excitement, and they have school tomorrow." She glanced up again to look at him. "What are you doing back here so late?"

Lifting his shoulder in a self-conscious shrug, he pushed away from the gate. "Came to check on the calf."

Reggie cocked her head, looking at him slyly. "Darn. And I was hoping this was that 'later' you promised earlier."

Cody's cheeks puffed as he blew out a long breath. Regan had always been bold, stating exactly what was on her mind instead of pussyfooting around an issue. Cody had always been a little slower, testing the waters a little before jumping in.

In spite of his hesitancy, he found himself chuckling as he remembered his frustration earlier that day—he hadn't been able to grab even a single second alone with her to make good on that promise.

"I never knew two kids could cover so much territory. Next time the high school needs chaperons for a dance, I'm volunteering Stephie and Jimmy. With those two little squirts around, those hormone-raging teenagers won't stand a chance of getting into any trouble."

Reggie bit back a smile. "I'm sure the high school students will thank you for your help."

Grinning, Cody crossed to hunker down in front of her and stretched out a hand to rub down the calf's side. "I talked to old man Peterson today. You remember him, don't you?" he asked, glancing up at her.

Reggie nodded her head. "Yes, he had a small farm down the road."

"Still does. I told him about our little friend here," Cody said with a nod toward the calf. "Seems he had a similar situation happen over at his place a couple of days ago, only he lost the calf, not the cow."

Reggie lifted her gaze, a puzzled frown pleating her forehead. "So?"

Cody lifted a shoulder. "I thought since he has a mama cow with milk and no baby to feed and we have a calf with no mama to feed it, we might put the two together.''

Reggie's eyes widened. ''You mean his cow could adopt our calf?''

A half grin tugged at the side of Cody's mouth as he pushed to his feet. ''Something like that.''

Reggie gently set the sleeping calf aside and rose, too. ''Oh, Cody! That would be wonderful!''

Cody held up a hand. ''Now don't get your hopes up. There's no guarantee that Peterson's cow will accept our calf.''

''But she might, right?''

He frowned, shaking his head. ''It's a possibility. A slim one,'' he reminded her.

''When can we get her?''

He glanced up. ''You mean you want to bring the cow here?''

''Well, sure— I can't ask Mr. Peterson to take on the responsibility for the animal. It's Harley's calf.''

Cody shook his head, grinning. ''In the morning. I'll take one of Harley's trailers over to Peterson's and haul her back over here.''

Unable to contain her excitement, Reggie grabbed his hands, squeezing them within her own. ''Oh, Cody. Thank you!''

Cody blushed, his cheeks turning a rosy pink. Laughing softly, Reggie rose to her toes and pressed a kiss to first one cheek, then the other. She sank back down, tipping up her face to smile at him. ''I'd forgotten how adorable you are when you're embarrassed. There's that little dimple that deepens on your left cheek.''

When the dimple deepened further, she tossed back

her head and laughed. Cody freed his hands to sling an arm around her shoulders, grateful for this new easiness between them. "Yeah, and you were always trying to embarrass me so you could see it," he replied as he guided her out of the stall. He stopped to close the gate and slide the lock into place. When he turned, she was watching him, her arms folded across her chest.

Her breasts rose and fell on a sigh. "It's good to be home, Cody." She glanced around the big barn, turning slowly. "I can't begin to tell you how much I've missed this place."

The sincerity and the regret in her voice touched something deep inside Cody's soul. He crossed to stand behind her, looping his arms around her waist. "You should never have left."

Sighing again, she leaned back against him, folding her arms over his. "I couldn't stay. Not with Susan here," she said, referring to Harley's first wife. "She hated me, though I never understood why."

"Susan had her own set of problems."

"True, but at the time I was afraid that her feelings for me would cause trouble between her and Harley."

Cody snorted. "Didn't seem to matter whether you were here or not. She left him anyway."

"Funny, isn't it?" she murmured as if to herself. "If I'd stayed, I would never have had to leave." She twisted her head around to look at Cody over her shoulder. "Does that make sense?"

"Yeah, with Susan gone, you'd have been happier."

No, Reggie thought sadly, knowing he was wrong. How could she have been happy once Cody had left

Temptation? She smiled wistfully, and turned to rest the back of her head on his chest again. "We had some good times in spite of her, though, didn't we?"

"Yeah, we did."

"Do you remember when you and Harley locked me in the feed room?" She felt the rumble of a laugh in his chest and gave his stomach a poke with her elbow. "It wasn't funny. I was scared out of my wits."

"We let you out," he reminded her.

"Yeah, after I promised to gather the eggs for a week."

He pressed his lips to her ear. "Never did like going in that henhouse."

Reggie chuckled, turning in his arms. "That's because the hens pecked you." She pressed the tip of a finger to his lower lip, teasing it open. "It takes a certain charm to persuade a female to give up something she holds dear."

"And I lacked that charm?"

She looked up at him, a slow smile teasing the corners of her mouth. "Oh, you had it all right. You just never thought to use it on the hens."

Fearing there was more behind her comments than just those hens, Cody frowned and caught her finger in his hand, drawing it from its sensual teasing. "If you're saying that I charmed you that night in the loft, you're—"

"No," she interrupted. "That was all my doing."

Cody hauled in a breath then slowly released it, wondering where this was going. "Regan," he began.

She pressed a finger to his lips, then stepped away from him, catching his hand in hers. "Come on," she whispered. "Let's see if our hideaway is still up there."

She pulled him along behind her as she headed for the wooden ladder that led to the loft overhead. At its base, she dropped his hand to curl her fingers around the ladder's side rails. Hooking a foot on the lowest rung, she hauled herself up. Cody stood beneath her, watching her ascent, his heart hammering in his chest, wondering what kind of heartbreak he was setting himself up for this time.

With a sigh, he climbed up after her, knowing that it didn't matter. He'd always been a fool for Regan.

When he stuck his head through the opening of the trap door he saw her standing in front of the open hay doors, her back to him. Moonlight silhouetted her shape, giving her an almost ethereal appearance and he wondered if this wasn't some dream that he'd wake from in the morning, as he had so many times in the past.

But then she turned, holding out a hand to him, just as she had once before, and he knew this wasn't a dream. This was Reggie, his Reggie, offering herself to him as freely, as innocently, as she had eleven years ago.

With emotion clotting his throat, he crossed to her, taking her hand in his. Though his face was shadowed, he could see her wistful smile, and knew that she was remembering, too.

"Reggie," he murmured, his voice husky. "Reggie," he said again as he drew her into his arms. He held her, his eyes pressed closed against the emotion that ripped through him, wanting the closeness that they'd once known yet wishing with all his heart that the years in between didn't exist.

Leaning back, she lifted her face to his in surprise. "Reggie," she whispered. "You called me Reggie. I've wanted to hear you say that."

"Why? You let everyone call you that."

Regan pressed a finger to his frowning lips. "I only allowed myself one memory when I left, and it was the sound of your voice calling me Reggie." She lifted her gaze to his. "Make love to me, Cody," she whispered. "In the moonlight like before."

Before he could respond, her fingers were reaching for the buttons of his shirt. Though he wished for the strength to say no to her as he should have done then, Cody couldn't find it. He'd never been able to deny Regan anything...except when she'd asked him to run away with her and marry her. At the time, he'd thought he'd made the right choice, the unselfish one. But he'd had years to regret that decision. He wouldn't live with any more regrets, he told himself.

His movements as hurried as hers, he jerked the shirt's hem from his jeans, working his way up the line of buttons while Regan worked her way down. Their fingers met somewhere in the middle, tangling briefly before she pushed the plackets aside. On a sigh, she pressed her lips against his bare chest. Softness. Tenderness. Heat. Each sensation ripped through Cody, until his head clouded, his knees weakened.

He dropped his head back on a low, guttural groan, grabbing at her wrists, needing something to hold on to. He felt her smile against his abdomen, felt her purr of sensual pleasure as she moved her lips lower, felt the scrape of her nails as her fingers sought the snap of his jeans.

"Reggie," he gasped, tightening his grip on her wrists.

"Sshhh," she whispered as the snap gave free.

Then her lips were on his again, nipping and teasing as her fingers made quick work of the zipper on his jeans. He groaned, taking her mouth with his, forcing her lips apart so that he could taste her sweetness. But tasting wasn't enough, he soon discovered. He needed to feel. He let go of her wrists to slip his hands beneath her blouse. Dipping his fingers in the waistband of her jeans at her back, he hauled her tight against him, pressing himself hard against her.

The action did nothing to satisfy the need that raged through him, but only added a new frustration to those that had haunted him all day, ever since she'd thrown herself into his arms in the pasture. Sliding his fingers along the waistband to the closure in front, he released the button with a pop that echoed in the cavernous loft, then eased down the zipper, letting his fingers drift over her heated flesh for a moment before he hooked his thumbs in the opening he'd created and stripped her of her jeans and panties.

Tearing his lips from hers, he stepped back, shucking off his shirt while he kept his gaze on her moonlit form. "You're beautiful, Reggie," he whispered. "More beautiful than I even remember."

He dropped the shirt to the loose hay behind him, then stepped to her, taking the hem of her own shirt in his hands. With a smooth upward lift, he carried it over her head, then dropped it, his gaze lingering on her bare breasts.

Silvered by moonlight, her breasts swelled beneath his gaze as she drew a shuddery breath. Slowly, almost reverently, he lifted a hand, taking the weight of a swollen globe in his palm...and felt the breath catch in her lungs. He shifted his gaze, meeting hers in the moonlight. He flicked a thumbnail across a nipple, then soothed with the pad of his thumb, watching as the heat built, turning her whiskey-colored eyes a deep umber. Her lids drifted shut and she arched, offering herself to him. Lowering his head, he touched his tongue to a nipple, teasing it into a tight bud with light velvet strokes.

"Cody," she murmured fervently, clutching at his hair. "I've wanted this, you, for so long."

She'd wanted him? Before Cody had a chance to absorb the words, her body was pressing intimately against his. On a groan, he stooped, catching her beneath the knees and scooping her up into his arms. He found her lips with his, tasting the heat, the need, and feeding it with his own. Dropping to a knee, he placed her on his spread shirt. Her hands lifted, reaching for him as he withdrew.

"Give me a minute," he murmured. Moving quickly, he kicked off his boots and stripped out of his jeans, then bent over her, planting his hands in the hay above her shoulders to support his weight as he lowered himself over her. Her arms locked around his neck, drawing him to her as he eased down. He shifted, nudging her thighs apart with his knees.

Reggie felt his manhood brush her, nearly screamed in frustration when he drew away. Then he returned, teasing her slowly, until she was breathless and clawing at his back. "Cody, please," she cried, arching against him.

"No, Reggie," he whispered, peppering her damp face with kisses. "We've waited a long time for this. We're going to make it last."

He tucked his head, laving a breast, then shifted again, dragging an arm between their damp bodies. He dipped a finger between her legs, wetting it with her honeyed sweetness, then teased back the velvet folds, exposing her feminine core. Again, and again he dipped into her, increasing the rhythm each time. Pleasure became pain, sweet and elusive as Reggie felt the first wave crest.

"Oh, Cody," she cried, clutching wildly at his back as the wave pulled at her, threatening to take her under.

"Ssshh," he soothed, covering her mouth with his. "Go with it. Let it take you."

The explosion came almost immediately. Cody felt its tremors as it shook her body. Gathering her close, he held her, whispering to her, covering her face with kisses. When at last she stilled, he moved over her again. "This one is for us," he whispered, pressing himself against her.

Sure that she didn't have the energy to respond, Reggie gasped when she felt the first hard thrust. Heat burned its way through her and she arched, instinctively taking him fully inside. He moved slowly, building the heat and the speed until she was breathless again, racing along with him.

Never had she known that passion had color, but it exploded behind her closed lids in jagged flashes like a kaleidoscope wildly shaken. Pleasure bordered on pain and yet she reached for it, even begged for it as she met each wild thrust.

She dug her fingers into Cody's back, feeling herself falling, but Cody was there to catch her. Holding her, taking her with him, as together they plunged over the edge into darkness.

Moonlight spilled across their naked bodies, adding an element of magic to an already mystical night. The dry, musty smell of hay mingled with the clean, sweet scent of country air wafting through the open hay door. Cody sighed, burying his nose in the damp hair at Regan's temple, reluctant to move, even more reluctant to leave her.

"I'm probably killing you," he murmured in apology. But when he tried to shift his weight from her, she clung.

"No, not yet," she whispered, lacing her fingers behind his neck. She forced her eyes open to look at him, wanting to remember this moment always. In the moonlight she could see that his face was still flushed with passion, his eyes still bright with a slowly fading heat. Damp hair feathered his forehead. With a soft smile curving at her lips, she finger-combed it back into place, then dragged that same finger lightly down his cheek to his jaw then stopped, pressing its tip at his chin.

The face was so familiar. Strong. Handsome. Endearing. She'd loved him as a girl, but those feelings were nothing compared to those she felt at the moment.

"Cody?"

"Hmm?"

"I—" She stopped, unsure of how he would respond if she shared her feelings with him. "Hold me," she whispered instead as she circled his neck with her arms again. "Please, just hold me."

The sound of metal striking metal drifted through Reggie's bedroom window and tangled in the web of her dream. She squeezed her eyes shut against the sound, clinging to the images that played through her mind. Cody. The hayloft. His body, slick with perspiration, poised above hers. His lips drifting down to meet hers. Pressure. Glorious pressure. A heat that threatened to burn.

Ping! Ping! Ping!

Groaning, she turned to her side, drawing her pillow over her head, trying to block out the intrusive sounds and hold on to the threads of the dream. But the sounds intensified, changing to an impatient hammering. Frustrated, Reggie squinted open an eye and peered at her bedroom window where dawn painted the sky pink.

Dragging herself from the bed, she padded barefoot to the window and pushed aside the drape. On the drive by the barn, she saw Cody's truck parked in front of one of Harley's trailers. He stood in the narrow space between the two, bent at the waist, hammering away at the hitch. As she watched, the hammering stopped and he straightened, shoving his hat back on his head. Using the crook of his elbow, he wiped at the sweat that beaded his brow before tossing the hammer into the back of the truck. He walked to the driver's side and opened the door. With one hand hooked on the top of the door, he turned, glancing in the direction of the house.

Reggie's fingers knotted in the drape's soft panels, as a sense of déjà vu swept over her. Cody had stood in almost that exact spot eleven years ago, the morning after they'd first made love. He'd come to see her, but she'd been too hurt, too angry at him for refusing to run away with her, to speak to him and had stubbornly refused to come outside. So she'd stood at her window hidden from view by the drapes and watched as he'd talked to Harley instead. As he'd prepared to leave, he'd turned, just as he had now, to glance at the house one last time before driving away. It was Harley who'd told her later that Cody had come to say goodbye, that he was leaving Temptation.

An unexplainable fear gripped Reggie, and she quickly grabbed her robe, pulling it on as she raced through the house. She palmed open the kitchen door, letting it slam behind her in her haste to catch Cody before he left.

"Cody! Wait!"

Cody snapped his head around at the sound of Regan's voice to see her racing across the lawn toward him, the tail of her robe whipping around her bare legs. As she neared, he saw the fear in her eyes and he quickly shouldered open the door and swung down.

"Regan, what's wrong?"

She stopped just short of reaching him, her chest heaving as she grabbed for each breath. "I was looking out my bedroom window and I saw you getting into your truck. And—" She gulped back tears, then pressed her hands at her cheeks, trying to find reason in this moment of madness. "I don't know," she moaned pitifully. "It was like before, watching you leave all over again. I had to stop you before it was too late."

Cody quickly closed the distance between them and caught her hands in his. "I'm not leaving, Regan. I'm just going down to Peterson's to get the cow."

She squeezed desperately at his hands, knowing how foolish she must sound, but unable to stop the stream of emotion that poured from her. "I was so scared I was going to lose you again. Everything was the same. Last night in the hayloft. Seeing you standing there this morning beside your truck." She shook her head, trying to clear the confusion, to separate the memories from the reality of the moment. "I know you must think me crazy, but this is all so difficult. Coming back after so many years, expecting everything and everyone to be just like they were when I left them." She lifted her gaze to his, her eyes glimmering with tears. "But they aren't, are they? Everything's changed."

"Not everything, Regan," he said softly, catching a tendril of hair to thread behind her ear. "I'll always be here for you, just like before."

She hauled in a shuddery breath, then forced a trembling smile as she caught his hand in hers and pressed it to her cheek. "I know. I just—" The tears came again, as unexpected as the terror that had swamped her only moments ago. She lifted her tear-filled eyes to him. "Hold me, Cody? Please?"

He slipped his arms around her, bringing her to his chest. Cupping a hand behind her head, he held her as she'd asked. She shifted, wrapping her arms at his waist, and snuggled close. Cody swallowed hard, suddenly aware that she wore nothing beneath the light robe.

The points of her breasts stabbed at his chest while the swell of her feminine mound pressed at his upper thigh. A sigh shuddered through her and Cody tightened his arms.

"You okay?" he asked.

Reggie stepped back, blotting her palms at her wet cheeks. "I'm fine now." She laughed then, if a bit self-consciously. "Though I'm sure you think I'm as crazy as a loon."

He caught her elbows, drawing her back. "You don't even want to know what I'm thinking," he said gruffly.

Surprised, Reggie flattened her palms against his chest to glance up at him. The heat in his eyes warmed her face, stirring to life a need that she thought they'd satisfied the night before in the barn.

"Cody Fipes," she said, her eyes widening in surprise. "It's barely six o'clock in the morning."

He dipped his head over hers, tracing the shape of her lips with his tongue. "And your point is?"

Reggie's lips parted on a sigh as heat raced through her. "What point?" she murmured as she lifted her arms to circle his neck.

Reggie pressed one hand to her forehead while keeping the receiver pressed to her ear with the other, already feeling the beginnings of a headache. She hadn't known how stressful getting two kids off to school could be. Jimmy hadn't been able to find his tennis shoes, Stephie had refused to eat the breakfast Reggie had prepared for them.

She frowned, remembering that particular little scene. Personally, she always ate fruit and dry toast for breakfast. How was she supposed to know that Mary Claire had turned into Martha Stewart after moving to Temptation and whipped up heart-shaped pancakes for the kids each morning for breakfast?

And to top it all off, while she'd been frantically mixing pancake batter, Cody had returned to deliver the cow to the calf. Feeling an obligation to help settle the cow in, she had dumped the batter on the griddle, instructed Jimmy to turn the pancakes when they bubbled and raced to the barn. She'd returned minutes later to find Stephie in tears, staring at a plate full of blackened pancakes.

Though tempted to go back to bed and bury her head under her pillow, she'd dried Stephie's tears and whipped up another batch of pancakes. Of course, by that time, the bus had come and gone. Thankfully, Cody had still been around and offered to take the kids to school.

And now she was alone…well, almost alone, she corrected herself, as she listened patiently to her secretary's update of the weekend activities at the office. Four new listings, six new sales to add to the books and a renter with an attitude. Behind her, the fax machine clacked away, spitting out paper.

This might be a vacation for Reggie, but she still had an office to run.

Sighing, she caught the receiver between her shoulder and ear and leaned back in Harley's chair to prop her bare feet on his desk.

"Call Mr. Johnson back," she instructed her secretary, "and tell him that we'll take care of the problem this time, but in the future, if his kids flush their toys down the toilet, he'll be responsible for the plumber's bill." She leaned forward to glance at her daily planner. "The termite inspection on the Tindale closing needs to be ordered," she reminded her secretary. "And you need to check with the mortgage company and see when their appraisers are scheduled. The owners want at least three days' notice."

The fax machine beeped, signaling the end of the transfer. Reggie dropped her feet and twisted around to gather the thick transmission from the machine. She scanned a few lines. "The contracts you faxed just arrived," she murmured absently into the phone as she read. "As soon as I have a chance to review them, I'll give you a call back. Oh, and, Marcy," she added, before hanging up, "call Murphy and light a fire under his butt. We need that change in zoning on the west Houston property approved by the end of the week."

Satisfied, she replaced the phone and picked up the contract her secretary had faxed her. Again lifting her bare feet to the top of Harley's desk, she settled back to read, a pen tucked behind her ear.

Cody watched from the doorway.

He'd never seen Regan in a business setting before and was having a hard time convincing himself that this no-nonsense woman who issued orders like a general to his troops was the same woman he'd discovered in the barn last night petting an orphaned calf. He found himself wishing for the other Regan, the more familiar one.

"Who's Murphy?"

Reggie jumped, then cursed when the papers she held slipped from her hands and scattered across the rug around her chair.

Cody chuckled as he stepped into the room. "Did I scare you?"

Reggie scowled, bending to scoop the dropped papers from the floor. "No, I always throw paper around just so I can pick it up again. Keeps me in shape."

Cody grinned as he hitched a hip on the edge of the desk and folded his hands over his thigh. He'd spent all morning at his office thinking about her, accomplishing nothing. Didn't seem to matter that he'd seen her only a few hours before. Thoughts of her muddled his mind, making work all but impossible. Cody glanced at the desk strewn with paper and sticky notes. It pained him a bit to know that Reagan didn't seem to suffer the same problem.

"Who's Murphy?" he asked again.

Reggie sorted through the papers, putting them back in order. "The zoning commissioner in Houston. I'm trying to get a property I have listed changed from residential to commercial and Murphy's dragging his feet."

"I thought you were supposed to be on vacation?"

Reggie tossed the stack of papers on the desk then sank back in the chair on a sigh. "I am, but I still have business to take care of."

Cody nodded as he picked up her daily planner. The day's page was crowded with tightly scrawled notations. For some reason, he discovered, that irritated him. "Want to have lunch with me?"

"I can't," she replied, her shoulders sagging with

real regret. "I have a teleconference with my sales force at twelve."

Cody drew a pen from his pocket as he scanned the appointment schedule. He had only a week with her, he reminded himself, and he intended to take full advantage. "Well, I'll be darned," he murmured. "Would you look at that? It's been cancelled," he said as he drew a bold line through the notation on the page.

Reggie lunged, grabbing for the book. Cody lifted it over his head, keeping it just out of reach. Reggie straightened and fisted her hands on her hips. "Cody Fipes," she warned. "You give me that book back right now."

"And what happens if I don't?"

"I'll—I'll—"

He tossed the book and the pen to the desk, but caught her hand as she reached for it, tugging her to stand between his spread knees. "You'll what?" he asked, cupping his hands beneath her buttocks, snugging her up against him.

Reggie puckered her lips in a pout. "You don't play fair," she complained halfheartedly as she plucked at the star on his chest. "Aren't you supposed to be busy upholding the law or something?"

"Or something," he replied huskily. He hooked a finger beneath her chin and tipped her face to his. "Have lunch with me. We'll whip up some sandwiches and take them up to Dead Man's Pass and have a picnic just like we used to."

Five

Reggie dropped the picnic basket onto the ground and plopped down beside it, burying her chin in her hands. "I still don't know how you managed to talk me into this. I've got work to do."

Cody chuckled. "It'll be there when you get back." He grabbed her hand and tugged her to her feet. "Let's go swimming."

"I don't have a suit," she grumped.

He tossed his hat to the blanket he'd spread on the ground, plucked his shirt from the waist of his jeans and began freeing buttons. "Ever heard of skinny-dipping?"

Reggie frowned at him as he peeled off his shirt. The fact that he suggested skinny-dipping wasn't what concerned her. It was the fact that she'd allowed Cody to talk her into canceling the teleconference with her sales force when she never, ever shirked her duties as owner and manager of the real estate company. For a woman who rarely took a day off, much less a vacation, this break from her normal routine was a little unsettling.

"Well?" he asked when she didn't move to join him. "What are you waiting for?"

Continuing to scowl, Reggie peeled her T-shirt over her head. "Marcy's going to think I've lost my mind," she muttered as she stooped to drag her shorts and panties down her legs. "Canceling a conference call at the last minute." With a huff of breath, she stepped out of the shorts and tossed them to the blanket. "And my sales force!" she continued to grouse, reaching her arms around to her back to fumble at the hook on her bra. "God only knows what they're thinking, or worse, what they're doing!" She stripped the straps down her arms and tossed the bra to the growing stack of clothes. "Phil's probably already on the golf course and I'd bet my last dollar that Barbara's shacked up in some motel with that lawyer she's been sneaking around with." She marched to the edge of the pool. "And it's all your fault," she muttered miserably as she stabbed a toe into the freezing water. "If you hadn't—"

Her scream split the air just before she hit the water, plunging beneath its icy depths. She rose, sputtering, scraping her hair from her face, to glare at Cody.

He dived over her head and surfaced behind her. "You were saying?" he asked, grinning as he tread water.

With an angry swipe of her hand, Reggie shot water in his face. He tossed back his head, laughing. "You're cute when you're mad."

"You'll think cute," she muttered, striking out toward him.

Cody stroked backward, staying out of reach. "Catch me if you can," he teased, then ducked below the water and disappeared from sight.

Frustrated, Reggie paddled in a circle, waiting for him to resurface. She squealed when something brushed her ankle, then sucked in a startled breath when she was yanked under. The water was crystal clear, and when she opened her eyes, she saw Cody in front of her. He grinned at her as he wrapped his arms at her waist and drew her to him. Bubbles of air drifted from his mouth as he closed it over hers...and Reggie forgot her anger, and gave herself up to the kiss.

His hands moved to cup her buttocks, drawing her more fully against him, and Reggie felt the swell of his manhood against her leg. Weightless, they drifted upwards, their lips still joined while the water pulsed around them, creating new sensations to add to those that already churned within them. They broke through the water simultaneously, still locked in each other's arms, gasping.

"Still mad?"

The work that awaited her forgotten, Reggie rubbed against him, enjoying the feel of his chest hair rubbing against her bare breasts. "I'm not sure."

He chuckled, taking her mouth with his. "Let me know when you've decided."

He kicked, taking her with him as he swam to a large limestone rock half submerged in the water.

Easing up on the ledge, he pulled her across his lap. Sunshine beat down on them, warming the chilled flesh exposed to the sun's rays. On a sigh, Cody gathered Reggie close, tucking her head in the curve of his neck. "Do you remember the last time we came up here on a picnic?"

Reggie smiled against his chest, threading her fingers through the hair there, remembering. "Yes, and as I recall we spent more time necking than we did eating."

Cody chuckled, smoothing a hand down her damp hair. "Yeah, we did." He shook his head. "I wanted to make love to you so bad that day I could taste it."

Reggie tipped her face to his. "Why didn't you?"

He reared back to peer down at her. "Well...because," he finished lamely.

"Because I was the boss's sister? Because you were afraid of what Harley would do to you if he caught us?"

Cody frowned, tucking her head back against his chest. "No, because I was three years older than you."

"Three years. Big deal."

"Yeah, it was a big deal," he replied defensively. "You were sixteen, jailbait, and I was nineteen, legally a man who was supposed to know better than to play around with innocent young girls."

"I'm not sixteen anymore, Cody," she reminded him, smoothing a hand across the flat plane of his stomach. "And I'm not innocent."

Cody sucked in a breath as her hand dipped lower. "No," he agreed, as the breath rattled out of him on a sigh. "You're not."

Regan moved to straddle him, bracing her hands on his shoulders. "We could make love now," she suggested as she dipped her head to catch the lobe of his ear between her teeth.

Shock waves ricocheted through his body as she closed her mouth over the lobe and suckled gently. "Yeah, I suppose we could," he said, his voice husky.

Smiling provocatively, Regan shifted again, bringing her body flush with his. Water lapped at Cody's waist at the movement. Beads of moisture glistened on her breasts in the bright sunshine, and Cody couldn't have resisted even if he'd wanted to. He dipped his head, licking at each crystal bead, savoring the taste and feel of her on his tongue, easing all the frustrations from that picnic long ago.

Her hips picked up the cadence of his mouth and moved against him, rubbing seductively at his thighs, at his groin. He felt himself harden, felt the heat of her feminine opening just out of reach, drawing him. Gathering her hips in his hands, he guided her to him, taking her mouth with his and swallowing the low moan of pleasure that escaped her lips at their joining.

"Reggie," he murmured, clutching her to him. "Oh, my God, Reggie," he groaned as he felt her velvet flesh close around him.

Time became unmeasurable, unimportant, as they moved together, increasing the rhythm and the speed until they both were gasping. Water surged around them, slapping at their heated flesh, adding its own sensual urgency to their lovemaking.

Unable to hold back any longer, Cody clutched her

hips to hold her to him. "Now, Reggie," he growled. "Now!"

Arching her head back, her body rigid, Reggie gave herself up to the delicious fists of pleasure that pummeled her. Replete, she sagged against him, wrapping her arms around his neck and finding his lips again.

A week, she thought as a wave of regret washed over her, dampening her eyes. How would she ever be able to leave Cody again?

Cody dropped his purchases on the counter of Carter's Mercantile.

Ruth Martin, the owner of Temptation's only grocery store, picked up a package of sirloin steaks to ring it up. "You hungry?" she asked dryly, noting the number of steaks in the package.

His thoughts centered on Regan and the evening he had planned, Cody looked at her in confusion. "What?"

With a scowl, Ruth waved the package of meat in front of his face. "Four steaks is a lot for one man."

"Oh," Cody replied, his cheeks warming. "They're not all for me. I'm cooking dinner tonight for Regan, Stephie and Jimmy."

Ruth pursed her lips, squinting at the numbers on the scale as she weighed a sack of potatoes. "Heard you were looking after things while Harley and Mary Claire were on their honeymoon. Thought it was just the livestock you were tending." She shot Cody a suspicious glance. "Didn't know you were feeding the humans, too."

Cody felt his face heat even more. Ruth Martin had a way of extracting information from a person that the FBI would envy, and she was better than a town crier at spreading what she unearthed.

"Just trying to be neighborly, is all," he replied vaguely.

Ruth pursed her lips, giving him a knowing look over the top of her smudged glasses. "That Regan is something, isn't she? Showing up after all these years."

Cody nodded his head, unsure what he was agreeing with. "Yeah, she's something all right."

"Done right well for herself from what I hear. Drives that fancy car and owns her own apartment complex in Houston, plus a real estate business." She didn't notice the tightening of Cody's lips at the mention of Regan's financial status. This was gossip and Ruth Martin was ready to share all she knew. "Did you know that that's where she met Mary Claire and Leighanna? The both of them leased apartments from her before moving here." She shook her head as she sacked Cody's purchases. "Small world, isn't it? Gets smaller every day."

"Yes, ma'am, it does," Cody murmured.

Ruth pushed the bag towards Cody. "Has she said anything about staying on after Harley and Mary Claire get back from their honeymoon?"

Cody shook his head, having a hard time pushing words beyond the lump in his throat that had formed at the mention of Regan leaving Temptation. "No, ma'am. I'm sure she'll need to get back home and tend to her business."

Ruth reared back, folding her arms beneath her breasts. "Home!" she said with a huff of breath.

"Can't imagine how anyone could call a hellhole like Houston home. Give me Temptation any day."

Because he tended to agree with her, Cody nodded his head.

"She could learn a thing or two from Mary Claire and Leighanna," Ruth continued in a matter-of-fact tone. "Those girls sure recognized a good thing when they saw Temptation. Paid off for 'em, too. Both found themselves good husbands here. If she put her mind to it, I bet Regan could find herself a husband, too." She gave her hand an impatient wave now that she had planted the seed she wanted to see sowed. "Would you listen to me? Here I am yapping my jaws and you've got steaks to cook. Get on now," she said, shooing Cody toward the door. "And be sure to tell those young'uns of Harley and Mary Claire's that I said hello."

Cody stood at the grill on the Kerrs' patio, his hands tucked beneath his armpits, staring out at the pasture where cows grazed in the growing dusk, thinking about what Ruth Martin had said about Regan.

If she put her mind to it, I bet Regan could find herself a husband, too.

She wouldn't have to look far, Cody thought on a wistful sigh. He'd be more than willing to take on the job. His chest tightened with emotion as the idea took shape in his mind. Regan and him married, buying land and building the house he'd always dreamed of. Having her to come home to every night. Sleeping with her, waking up with her, sharing the events of his days.

But would Regan consider staying in Temptation? he wondered. He'd never really considered the possibility. He'd always assumed that she'd go back to Houston once Harley and Mary Claire returned home from their honeymoon.

He gave himself a firm shake and turned to pick up the fork. *You're a damn fool, Cody Fipes, to even think such a damn fool thing,* he told himself sternly as he stabbed the fork into a steak and turned it. *Why would Regan want to stay in a two-bit town like Temptation when everything she's worked toward for the last ten years is in Houston?*

"A penny for your thoughts?" Regan whispered as she wrapped her arms around his waist from the back.

Cody shook his head, frowning. "If I had one worth anything, you could have it and keep your penny."

Regan chuckled, then pressed her lips to his spine. "You never did have much faith in your own worth."

Cody tossed down the fork in disgust. "That's because I'm not worth much. I'm just a two-bit sheriff in a two-bit town."

Surprised by the anger in his reply, she stepped around him, leaving one arm wrapped at his waist as she peered up at him. "Where did this blue mood come from?"

Cody struggled to push back the anger, the frustration. He wouldn't ruin what time he had left with her by feeling sorry for himself. He dipped his head to press a kiss on her mouth. "Just stating the facts." He glanced over her head. "Where are those kids? The steaks are almost ready."

"They're in their rooms doing their homework.

Cody," she persisted, not wanting to drop the subject. "Don't you realize how talented you are? You're good at so many things."

"Like what?" he asked in disgust.

"Well, for starters, you're a three-time-world-champion bull rider."

That she was aware of his wins surprised Cody. He frowned, ducking his chin to peer at her. "How did you know that?"

Reggie shrugged, embarrassed to admit she'd followed his rankings all those years. "We do get the news in Houston," she replied vaguely. Hoping to refocus the conversation on him and not her, she added, "Winning those championships took a lot of determination, a lot of skill. Not many men can claim that level of success."

Cody stared at her, seeing the earnestness in her expression, that defiant gleam in her eyes. That she would defend him, even to himself, touched him deeply. But he knew she was wrong. Cody Fipes didn't have anything to offer to anybody, least of all to Regan.

A week, he reminded himself. That's all the time he had to gather up enough memories to last him a lifetime.

Turning to face her, he draped his arms low at her waist, drawing her to him. "Thanks. If I ever have need of a publicist, I'll call you." Forcing a smile, he dipped his head over hers.

"Kissy, kissy, kissy," Stephie sang in a singsongy voice.

Reggie tore her mouth from Cody's to find Stephie standing not six feet away. "You're supposed to be in your room doing your homework, young lady," she said sternly, trying to hide her embarrassment at having been caught kissing Cody.

Stephie held up a paper, waving it in the air. "I finished. I just need somebody to call out my spelling words for me."

On a sigh, Cody dipped his head over Regan's again for a quick kiss. "I'll handle this one," he murmured before releasing her. "Okay, squirt, looks like I'm your man," he said, turning to Stephie.

Her eyes lit up and she skipped across the patio and jumped into Cody's arms. He caught her, hitching her to one hip. "Now these aren't big words, are they?" he asked, as he moved to sit on the swing.

"Really big ones," Stephie warned, settling in his lap as she smoothed the paper across her knees. "The first one is..." She struggled a moment, trying to sound out the word. "Huh—ow—sss."

Cody took the paper from her, squinting at the short list of first-grade words. "House," he repeated. "Can you spell it?"

Stephie cocked her head to beam a smile at him. "H—O—U—S—E," she said proudly.

Cody popped a kiss on the top of her head. "Well, that's really good, squirt. How about this one? Waa—gon," he said, sounding the word out phonetically for Stephie's benefit.

Reggie watched them, her arms folded across her breast. *And he thinks he isn't good at anything,* she thought with a shake of her head. *He's patient and kind and loving. He'll make a wonderful father some day.*

A sigh moved through her at the thought. Cody, a

father. Though his own father hadn't provided much
of an example, she knew that Cody would make a
good one. She'd seen evidence enough in his inter-
actions with Jimmy and Stephie to convince her that
he knew how to dole out the equal portions of dis-
cipline and love that children needed. She could see
him with a babe in his arms and bouncing another on
his knee.

Sadness washed over her as the image built, and
she quickly pushed away the thought and headed for
the kitchen to check on the potatoes Cody had put in
the oven to bake.

Though he tried to hide it, Reggie could see that
Cody's blue mood persisted, and she wondered about
it as they sat together on the patio swing in compan-
ionable silence. Stars winked above them, scattered
across a sea of black velvet. A quarter moon, looking
like a sliver of gold in the dark sky, hung suspended
above a huge live oak tree. Frogs croaked from a
distant pond.

Reggie gathered her knees tighter to her breasts and
inched closer to Cody, hoping to revive the carefree
mood they'd shared at Dead Man's Pass that afternoon. His arm tightened around her, drawing her
close, but he remained silent, staring off into space.

"Thanks for cooking dinner for us," she said, hoping to draw him into conversation. "If not for you,
the kids would have had to settle for bologna sandwiches."

When he didn't reply, she gave him a poke in the
ribs. "Cody!"

He whipped his head around to stare at her. "What?"

She huffed an impatient breath. "Nothing. I was just making sure you weren't sleeping."

He lifted his hands above his head, stretching. "I'm not asleep," he said, then dropped his arm back around her shoulders. "Just thinking."

She snuggled close again. "About what?"

He dipped his chin, meeting her gaze. "You."

Warmth spread through Reggie's body and she smiled up at him. "What were you thinking?"

There was no way Cody could tell her what he was truly thinking about, so he hedged. "Sure you want to know?"

"Well, of course I do!"

"I was just thinking about how much your boobs have grown since you were seventeen."

Reggie reared back and socked him hard in the arm. "Cody Fipes! I can't believe you said that!"

He rubbed at his arm, chuckling. "You asked."

Reggie flopped around on the swing, folding her arms beneath her breasts. "Well, I'm sorry now that I did."

He draped his arm around her again and tried to draw her back to his side, but Reggie refused to soften. "Bigger's not bad," he murmured softly. "In fact, I kinda like the change."

She pressed her lips firmly together, refusing to be coddled.

"Ahh, Reggie," he murmured, nuzzling his nose at her ear. "Don't be mad."

Reggie felt herself weakening. "A few things have

gotten bigger on you, too," she said, not willing to forgive him just yet.

Cody glanced down at his stomach, knowing that he'd put on some weight over the years. "Like what?"

"Wel-l-l," she said pointedly, dropping her gaze to his fly.

Cody's eyes bugged and his face reddened...then he tossed back his head and laughed. To Reggie, it was the sweetest music she could hear. Finally—if unintentionally—she'd managed to pull him from the dark mood he'd been in all night.

Hooking an arm around her neck, he pulled her down, rubbing his knuckles against her head like he had when they were kids. "Your mind's in the gutter."

Laughing, Reggie struggled to get free. "You should talk. Bigger boobs," she admonished, shoving back her hair when he released her.

Cody grinned, cupping a breast in his hand and running a thumb across a nipple. "Yeah, but men are supposed to notice things like that."

"And women aren't?"

Cody lifted his hands in surrender. "Now don't start burning your bra just yet. I was only teasing."

Reggie sniffed indignantly, tugging her shirt back into place after their tussle. "You better be. I've taken down stronger men for less."

Cody arched a brow, appraising her. "I'll just bet you have."

"I have. A single woman in a large city has to know how to take care of herself."

"You could leave, you know." The suggestion was out of his mouth before he could stop himself.

Reggie's mouth dropped open. "Leave Houston?" She sputtered a laugh. "And where would I go?"

"Temptation's a good town."

"But what would I do here? How would I support myself?"

Cody's frown returned. "It was just a suggestion."

A shiver chased down Reggie's spine as she stared at Cody. She'd never thought about staying in Temptation. She'd thought plenty about leaving when her week was up, already aware of how much she'd miss Cody when she left. But she'd never considered staying.

"Cody," she began softly, reaching to lay a hand on his sleeve.

At her touch, he bolted from the swing like he'd been launched from it. "Forget I mentioned it. It was a stupid idea." He grabbed his hat from the patio table and shoved it on his head. "I need to get going. I've got to be at work early in the morning."

Stunned by his hasty departure, Reggie sat on the swing, watching him as he strode toward his truck, and wondered what she'd said that set him off.

Two days passed without Reggie seeing Cody. On Tuesday and Wednesday he made his visits to the farm as he'd promised Harley, but he made them early in the morning while Reggie was getting the kids ready for school, or timed them late in the evening when she was busy getting dinner on the table and supervising Jimmy and Stephie while they did their homework.

Never once did he approach the house.

Reggie stewed the full two days, wondering what she'd done, what she'd said that had upset him.

She reached the end of her patience on Thursday, the third morning of his absence, when she saw Stephie standing at the kitchen window watching Cody drive away.

"How come Cody never comes to see us anymore?" Stephie asked, her chin quivering. "Did we do something to make him mad?"

Right then and there, Reggie decided to put an end to this foolishness. "Come on, kids," she said, fighting back her own anger. "I'm taking you to school this morning."

After dropping them off, she headed for Main Street and Cody's office, determined to find out the reason for his absence. She pulled into the space in front of the jailhouse, parking her Lexus alongside his truck. She ducked her head to peer through the windshield and stared at the office, wondering what kind of reception she should expect.

The front of the building was weathered, the sign proclaiming "Sheriff's Office" faded to a dull gray. A long jagged crack ran from one corner of the plate glass window to another. Grass grew between the cracks in the sidewalk out front.

I'm nothing but a two-bit sheriff in a two-bit town.

Cody's words of self-condemnation came back to her. Was that what was wrong with him? she wondered. Was he dissatisfied with his life in Temptation and his job?

On a sigh, she climbed from her car. It wouldn't

do any good to second-guess his bad mood. It was better to ask him outright.

She didn't bother to knock, but twisted open the door and stepped inside, pausing a moment to let her eyes adjust to the change in light.

The office was small and stark. A gun-metal-gray desk sat at an angle to the front door, four file cabinets of a similar color lined the wall behind it. Two chairs, one that listed decidedly to the left, were positioned in front of the desk.

On an opposite wall, a beat-up table held a coffee-pot and a computer, Temptation's one concession to technology. Above it a bulletin board hung, covered with thumbtacked "Wanted" posters. A closed door led to the back where, Reggie knew, there was a single cell and beyond it, Cody's living quarters.

But Cody was nowhere in sight.

Feeling as if she was trespassing, Reggie took a timid step into the room. "Cody?" she called softly. When he didn't answer, she moved toward his desk. A wooden frame on the corner caught her eye and she picked it up. The photo was of Cody riding Bodacious, the rankest bull on the rodeo circuit. She remembered seeing the same picture in the Houston *Chronicle* the year Cody had won his first world title.

The photographer had snapped the shot when Bodacious had begun his famous spin. Cody was leaning back against the gloved hand cinched tight in the rosined bull rope while his free arm arced the air in front of him, fighting to stay in the center of the spin. His hat was pulled low over his eyes, but Reggie could see the intensity of his expression, the determination in the set of his jaw. She remembered crying when she'd seen the picture in the paper, proud of him for the win and wishing with all her heart that she could have been there to congratulate him.

The front door opened behind her and Reggie spun, the picture still clutched in her hand, to see Cody step across the threshold. Their eyes met and held a full three seconds before he closed the door behind him.

Reggie held up the picture. "Eight seconds. It must have been a hell of a ride."

Cody took the picture from her and replaced it on the corner of his desk. "What are you doing here?"

Reggie refused to let his gruff tone affect her. She'd come to find out what had happened and she wasn't leaving until she did. "I came to see where you work."

She turned slowly, as if inspecting the office for a prospective client. "Nice place. Compact but orderly." She walked to the computer and pressed a key. "And all the newest technology."

"What do you want, Regan?"

She turned to find him leaning against the front of his desk, his arms folded across his chest. The silver star on his pocket caught the sunlight coming through the window and shot a bead of light on the opposite wall.

"Nothing really. Just dropped by to say hello." She moved to stand beside him, her shoulder brushing his, and fingered the papers that littered his desk. "Nice filing system," she murmured.

Cody grabbed her hand, his fingers closing like a vise around her wrist. Reggie snapped up her head, her gaze hitting his. She could see the anger in his eyes and felt her own bubble to the surface.

"What do you want, Regan?"

She tipped up her chin, ready to do battle. "I want to know what happened. Why you haven't dropped by the house when you come out to the ranch to check on the cattle."

Cody bit back an oath and pushed away from the desk to move behind it. "I'm busy, Regan. I've got a job to do." He picked up a fistful of papers and shuffled through them.

Refusing to let him get rid of her so easily, Reggie remained in front of the desk. "You found time on Monday."

Cody tossed the papers to his desk, planting his hands on top of them as he glared at her across the width of the desk. "What do you want from me, Regan? Blood?"

Stunned by the fury in his reply, Reggie could only stare. "I don't want anything from you that you're not willing to give. I—I thought we were friends."

"Friends?" Cody repeated, his voice rising. "We're more than friends, Regan. We're lovers."

She swallowed hard, lifting her chin. "Yes, we are."

"And what happens when your week is up? What happens when you go back to Houston?" He came around the desk to stand in front of her, his hands braced low on his hips. "What then, Regan?"

"I—I don't know," she murmured, her gaze held by the anger in his. "I suppose we will see each other occasionally. You could come to visit me in Houston and I could come to Temptation to see you."

Cody lifted his hands to cover his face, then dragged them through his hair. "Visits," he repeated, then lifted his gaze back to hers. "Is that enough for you?"

"Will it be enough for you?" she challenged in return.

She watched the emotion play across his face, the tightening of his jaw, the vein at his temple that pulsed to life, and understood the war that was going on inside him. She understood because she was battling the same emotions, the same confusion at the thought of leaving him.

Slowly, the fight drained from him. "I don't know," he murmured, dropping his eyes.

She took a step closer, finding the courage to lay a hand on his arm. This time he didn't flinch away. Instead, he caught her shoulders and hauled her into his arms. "Oh, Regan. What are we doing?" he asked on a low groan.

She looped her arms around his waist and squeezed, fighting back tears. "We're taking advantage of what time we have together, that's what." She sniffed and pushed from his arms. "Now you listen to me and listen good. I expect you for dinner tonight, and I'm not accepting any excuses." She brushed her fingers beneath her eyes, then lifted her face to his, cocking her head at a determined angle. "And I'm warning you, if you're not there by seven, I'll come looking for you."

Before he could refuse her, she turned and marched for the door. She paused, her hand on the handle, and looked back at him.

"Oh, and Cody," she said, her voice softening. "I'm planning something really special for dessert."

Six

After leaving Cody's office, on impulse Reggie dropped by the barbershop, hoping to talk Will Miller, Temptation's only barber, into cutting her hair before she headed back to the ranch.

When the bell clanged over the door, announcing her arrival, Will glanced up from the head of hair he was trimming. His eyes widened in surprise when he saw her. "Well, if it isn't Regan Kerr in the flesh."

Reggie smiled. "Giles," she corrected.

"Kerr. Giles. Don't matter. You're still our little Regan. What can I do for you today?"

Reggie's smile deepened at the "little" tag before her name. She supposed that no matter how she much she aged, she'd still be considered Harley's "little" sister and the town's "little" Regan. It had been so ten years ago when she'd left Temptation, and seemed to still hold true today.

"I need a trim. Have you got time?"

Will bobbed his chin, turning his attention back to the customer in the chair. "I'll be right with you. Soon as I finish lowering old Dick's ears."

Reggie crossed to the chairs that lined the wall of the narrow shop and dropped down, plucking a magazine from the pile scattered on the small table beside her. Absently she flipped the pages, thinking about her conversation with Cody.

We're more than friends. We're lovers. She sighed, understanding his frustrations. Yes, they were lovers, but he lived in Temptation and she in Houston. What else could they do but take advantage of what time they had available to them? She had her business, her investments and Cody had his job as sheriff. Neither could walk away easily. She toyed with the idea of Cody resigning as sheriff and moving to Houston to be near her...but quickly dismissed the idea. Cody would smother in a city as crowded as Houston. He needed the wide-open spaces and the slower pace that Temptation offered.

She was nearly halfway through the publication when she realized that she was staring at a picture of the man who occupied her thoughts.

Cody in *People* magazine? she asked herself in surprise as she folded the magazine in half to the study the picture. He stood in front of his office, his arms folded across his chest. That he wasn't comfortable posing for the camera was obvious in the sullen slant of his mouth, the impatience in his stance.

Settling back, she began to read and soon lost herself in the accompanying article.

A gnarled finger thumped the page. "See you're readin' about our local star," Will said, chuckling.

Reggie lifted her head. "This is unbelievable." She closed the magazine, noting that the date was months ago.

Will waved her to the chair. "Come on, let's get to cuttin' before Marvin comes in for his shave."

Reggie laid the magazine aside and rose, following him. "You know, I saw a blurb on the news one night several months ago about Temptation, but I had no idea that y'all had received so much national attention."

Will propped his foot on the chair's lever and pumped. "Yep. Old Cody drew the spotlight right to us."

Reggie met his gaze in the mirror. "Were things really that bad for Temptation?"

"Worse," he muttered, frowning. "They were considerin' shuttin' down our high school and sendin' the kids over to a neighboring town for their schoolin'. Businesses were closin' right and left." He shook his head sadly. "Yeah, it was that bad."

"Has Cody's suggestion to save Temptation worked? I mean, are people really moving here?"

Will's chest swelled proudly. "Hell, yes, they're movin' here!" He laid a hand on her shoulder, immediately contrite. "Sorry, Regan. Didn't mean to cuss. Harley'd skin me alive if he knew I spoke that way in front of you."

Biting back a smile, Reggie patted his hand. "That's okay, Will. I won't tell."

Obviously relieved, Will whipped a plastic drape around Reggie and snapped it behind her neck as he returned to his story. "Had a couple move in a few months back that are openin' a clothin' business. Right now they're remodelin' the store, puttin' in fixtures and such. Others are coming, as well. Got us a builder whose gonna put up some houses on what used to be the old Gantt place. We're hopin' a plumber'll move in soon. Lost the only one we had about six months ago." He picked up his scissors. "We're not out of the woods, yet, but things are lookin' up." He dipped his face near her ear, looking at her reflection in the mirror. "Now how much you wantin' me to take off, sweetheart?"

Her mind churning with thoughts of Temptation dying and Cody's efforts to save it, Reggie replied absently, "Just the ends."

Steam from the boiling pot of water rose to mist Reggie's cheeks as she dumped the pasta shells into the colander she'd placed in the sink, her thoughts focused on her conversation with Will Miller. Setting the pot aside, she quickly doused the shells with cold water.

Close the high school? She shuddered at the possibility as she began to mix the filling for the shells. She'd graduated from that high school, as had Harley and Cody before her, and she couldn't bear the thought of it closing down. It was a wonderful school, small enough to cater to the individual needs of its students but large enough to offer a quality education. It was staffed with local people who sincerely cared about the students they taught.

Surely there's something that can be done! she fretted as she shredded parsley. There had to be more ways to entice people to— She stopped, her fingers freezing on the sprig of parsley, as a solution popped into her head.

"Benning!" she whispered. He wanted to relocate his manufacturing business from Houston to a smaller town and Reggie had spent hours studying the demographics of possible sites for her client. Why not Temptation? she asked herself. It certainly met his requirements. Low taxes, friendly community, good schools. And if he chose Temptation, he'd bring a hundred employees with him. What a boom that would bring not only to Temptation's population but to its economy, as well!

Excited now, she grabbed a spoon and stirred the cheese mixture, blending in the parsley. She'd run it by Cody, she promised herself, just as soon as he arrived for dinner. At the thought, she rested her spoon against the side of the bowl and lifted her head to stare out the window.

Would he think her idea a good one? she wondered. Cody, like the other residents of Temptation, liked their town just the way it was and might resent her meddling. She gave herself a firm shake. Of course he'd like it, she told herself. They wanted growth, and an addition of one hundred families to their present population would go a long way in fulfilling that need.

Reggie heard Cody's truck on the drive and glanced at the clock. Seven o'clock, right on the dot. She bit back a smile as the back door opened behind her, glad to know that he'd responded to her invitation and she wouldn't have to go looking for him as she'd threatened.

"Hello?"

"Come on in!" Reggie called as she bent to pull the bread from the oven.

"Boy! Something sure smells good."

Reggie straightened, her heart tipping crazily at the sight of him standing in the middle of the kitchen, his hat in his hands. He'd changed his clothes since she'd seen him at his office that morning and had obviously taken the time to shower and shave. His hair was still a little damp at the ends and held the crease of his hat. She let her gaze wander over him, taking in the crisp blue shirt, which turned his gray eyes blue, the starched jeans and the polished boots before returning to his face.

He looked a little uncomfortable, but Reggie figured that was understandable, considering their conversation that morning.

Hoping to put him at ease, she crossed to him to brush a kiss on his cheek. "I hope it tastes as good as it smells. My culinary skills tend toward takeout."

Cody chuckled, following her. "What can I do?"

"You can set the table."

A frequent visitor in the Kerr home, Cody knew where everything was kept. He gathered plates, silverware and napkins and carried them to the table, carefully laying them out just as Mrs. Kerr had taught him years before.

"What are we having?" he asked as he aligned the silverware at each place.

"Manicotti," Reggie replied as she sat a steaming

casserole on the table. She glanced up to smile at him. "I hope you like it."

Manicotti? Cody didn't know whether he liked it or not. He was more a meat-and-potatoes man himself. "Never had it, but it sure smells good."

The door from the den swung open and Stephie raced into the kitchen. "Cody!" she squealed. She jumped, knowing he would catch her, and wrapped her arms around his neck. Popping a kiss on a cheek, she leaned back, puckering her lips in a pout. "Where've you been? I've missed you."

Cody met Reggie's gaze over the top of Stephie's head. She arched a brow, letting him know that he wouldn't get any help from her end. "Fightin' crime," he replied, shifting his gaze back to Stephie's. "How did you do on that spelling test we studied for?" he added, hoping to distract her.

"I made a hundred."

Cody gave her a hug. "That's my girl. I knew you could do it."

Not one to be easily diverted, Stephie placed a hand on Cody's cheek and forced his face to hers. "There's no crime in Temptation. Mama told me so herself. So why'd you really stay away? Did Aunt Reggie make you mad or something?"

Heat flamed in Cody's cheeks and once again he shifted his gaze to Regan's. This time, thankfully, she took pity on him.

"No, darling," she answered for him. "We just had a misunderstanding, is all."

"You had a fight," Stephie stated in a matter-of-fact voice. "Mama and Harley had a fight once and he bought her a horse so she would forgive her."

She looked back at Cody. "Did you buy Aunt Reggie a horse?"

Cody tried his best not to laugh. He dug his fingers into Stephie's ribs, making her giggle. "No, squirt, I don't think your aunt would have much use for a horse in Houston."

"So how'd you get her to forgive you?"

Cody sighed, looking at Regan. "I'm not sure that she has yet."

Reggie saw the uncertainty in his eyes and it touched her heart in a way that an apology never could. "There was nothing to forgive," she told Stephie, reaching to take the child from Cody's arms. "It was a misunderstanding, just like I said, and now it's over." She set Stephie on the floor and gave her backside a soft swat. "Now, scoot and get your hands washed. Dinner's almost ready."

Reggie laced her fingers through Cody's as they strolled across the lawn in the moonlight. Dinner was over, the kitchen clean and Jimmy and Stephie fast asleep in their beds. At last, she had Cody all to herself.

"Has the cow taken to the calf?" Cody asked.

Reggie smiled softly. "Like it's her own. I only had to bucket-feed the calf that first day. Since then the cow has let her nurse."

Cody twisted his head to look at her, one eyebrow cocked. "This I've got to see."

"All right. Follow me." Reggie led him into the barn and to the stall where the cow and calf were kept. Together, they braced their arms along the top of the gate and leaned to peer inside. The cow stood patiently in the far corner while the orphaned calf, his legs braced wide, nursed noisily.

"Well, I'll be darned," Cody murmured, watching. "She *has* taken to him."

Reggie smiled, dropping her chin onto her hands. "Yes, they both seem pretty content." She turned a cheek to the back of her hand to peer up at Cody. "Do you think we can turn them out in the pasture with the others soon?"

He curved a hand around her shoulder and hugged her to his side as he shifted his gaze back to the cow. "Don't know why we can't. I'll take care of it first thing in the morning."

"Can I help?"

Cody grinned down at her. "Think you're ready for a trail drive, huh?"

Reggie straightened, laughing, to wrap her arms at his waist. "A trail drive, consisting of one cow and a five-day-old calf. I think I can handle it."

Cody looped his hands behind her neck, dipping his head to brush his nose against hers. "Then it's a date."

"You'll have to wait until I get the kids off to school," Reggie warned. "Things are pretty hairy around here until they leave."

"No problem."

Remembering the idea that had come to her earlier that day, she slipped her hands from his waist and caught his hand. "Let's go sit out on the patio."

After they had retraced their steps back to the house, Reggie settled in the middle of the porch swing Harley had built for Mary Claire, leaving just enough room for Cody to slip in beside her.

Once he'd settled, she curled her legs beneath her and rested her head against his shoulder and laid a hand on his chest. Crickets chirped their night song somewhere in the darkness, while a cow lowed in a distant field. Though the sounds usually soothed Reggie, tonight she didn't even hear them. Her mind was focused on the idea she wanted to share and wondering how best to present it to Cody.

"Cody," she said hesitantly, "I've been thinking."

"About what?"

"Well," she began. "I was in the barbershop today and I saw the copy of *People* magazine. You know, the one with your picture and the story about your idea to save Temptation?"

Cody frowned. He remembered all too well the article she was referring to. He'd suffered through a year's worth of teasing over the picture alone. "Yeah, I know the one," he replied dryly.

"Well, it started me thinking." She lifted her head and twisted around on the swing to face him, needing to monitor his response to the idea. "I have a client in Houston," she explained. "A manufacturer, who's looking for a place to relocate his business. He isn't particular about location, just so long as he can escape the current taxes he's forced to pay."

Cody's forehead pleated into a frown. "You're thinking of sending him to Temptation?"

"Yeah," she said, releasing a nervous breath. "But only if you think it's a good idea. The man designs and manufactures furniture and is environmentally friendly," she hastened to add, "so you wouldn't need to worry about him polluting the air or the water around Temptation. He'd need about twenty acres to build his plant on and probably another twenty for future expansion. Right now he employs about a hundred people, most of whom I'm sure would be willing to make the move with him. And his expansion plans for 250 employees in five years. If he decided to build his plant here, it would certainly give Temptation the boost in population that you've wanted.''

"I suppose it would," he replied hesitantly. "But we're a rural community. We don't have the businesses to support that kind of growth."

Since he didn't immediately put a nix on her idea, she hurried to explain. "That's the beauty of this. Most of the employees have families. They'd be bringing children to enroll in your schools, and spouses who would probably need jobs, as well. I'm sure several of them would see the opportunity here and perhaps want to open businesses of their own. Plus, other people would hear of Temptation's sudden burst in population and would flock here in hopes of cashing in on the escalating economy."

Cody lifted his gaze to stare at her. "But where would they live? Temptation doesn't have much of a real estate market."

"I've already thought of that. When I was at the barber shop earlier today, Will mentioned that a developer was going to build a tract of houses on the old Gantt place. If my client decided to move his business here, we could talk to that developer and arrange for him to build houses within the price range of the employees who would be moving here, plus maybe even an apartment complex or two."

"An apartment complex," Cody repeated, having a hard time imagining it all.

"Yes, and that's not all. With all the new growth, the existing businesses would see an upsurge in revenue and there would be a need for *more* businesses. A dry cleaner's, more restaurants, maybe even a McDonald's!"

Cody had never seen Regan like this. She was like a child with a new toy. Her eyes were bright with excitement, her body pulsing with an energy she was having a hard time containing. He imagined that she would look much like this when working a deal at her office in Houston. He quickly pushed away the thought, not wanting to imagine Regan anywhere but right there in Temptation.

"Do you really think your client would consider Temptation?" he asked doubtfully. "We're sorta off the beaten path."

"Of course he would! I wouldn't have mentioned it otherwise."

Cody blew out a long breath, not at all sure he— or Temptation, for that matter—was ready for a boom to their economy of this magnitude. "You'll want to play this by the mayor first, but I guess it wouldn't hurt any to give the man a call to see if he's interested."

She threw her arms around Cody's neck. "I just knew you would agree!"

Chuckling, Cody gathered her close. "Are you always like this when you get a bee in your bonnet?"

She drew back to cup his cheeks in her hands. "Yes!" she said, then laughed. "Putting together a deal just turns me on."

Cody drew back a fraction. "Turns you on?" he repeated.

She shifted, drawing her feet underneath her to kneel while she faced him, amused at the wary look in his eye. "Yeah," she said, drawing the single word out in a sultry drawl. "I love the challenge," she purred and plucked open the first two buttons on his shirt. With her gaze on his, she slipped a hand inside and gently scraped her nails down his chest. "The negotiations," she murmured huskily, leaning to nip at his lips. "And bringing together all the ends that need to be tied up to close a deal." She shifted again, moving to straddle him on the swing.

"Lord, have mercy," Cody whispered.

She smiled against his lips. "Remember that dessert I promised you?"

Cody was having a hard time remembering his name, much less any promises. "Y-yeah," he stammered. "Maybe."

"Well, this is your dessert."

The next morning Reggie sat behind Harley's desk, the phone receiver pressed between shoulder and ear while she scribbled notes on an already filled legal pad. "Temptation is perfect for you, Cal. Low taxes, lots of room for expansion, friendly people, an all but nonexistent crime rate. The town itself looks like a Norman Rockwell painting, kind of sleepy but that's its charm.

"Picture this," she told him as she reared back in her chair, templing her fingers in front of her as she built her own mental image. "There's one main street that runs through the center of town where most of the businesses are located. An American flag flies over the grocery store, which does double duty as the post office. The original striped pole still turns slowly at the entrance to the barber shop. The only traffic is a farm truck chugging down the street. People stroll down the sidewalk at a leisurely pace, unafraid of being mugged or hit on by some panhandler.''

Cal chuckled. "Sounds like heaven. Are you familiar with the locals?"

A sound had Reggie glancing up. Cody stood in the doorway, his hat in his hands.

"Very," she replied to Cal as she motioned for Cody to join her. "I grew up in Temptation."

"When can I look the place over?"

She scraped papers out of the way so that Cody could prop a hip on the corner of the desk. "At your convenience. I'm in Temptation now, but plan to return to Houston sometime this weekend. Of course, I can rearrange my schedule to suit yours."

"Hold on a minute while I check my calendar."

Reggie pressed a hand over the mouthpiece. "It's Cal Benning," she whispered to Cody. "The man I told you about last night. He's checking his calendar to see when he can come and look over Temptation." She raised a hand, crossing two fingers, and held her breath as she waited for Benning to return to the line. She could imagine him digging through the reams of designs that always cluttered his desk, in search of the elusive calendar.

"Won't work this weekend or next week," she heard him mutter. "I'm scheduled to make a trip to North Carolina. And the Dallas Market opens the week after. How about the first of November?"

More than three weeks away, Reggie thought, biting back a groan of disappointment. Impatient to get things rolling, she had to force a smile into her voice as she replied, "That'll be great. I'll send your secretary a map with directions and set up a meeting for you and Temptation's mayor."

Replacing the receiver, she let out a sigh. "He can't get here for three weeks. He's planning on coming the first of November."

Cody nodded his head slowly, wondering if she would be making the trip with him. "I suppose we can wait that long."

She smiled, leaning to place a hand on his thigh. "You don't sound very excited. Having second thoughts?"

Cody gave his head a quick shake, not wanting to dwell on the thought of Regan returning...or leaving, for that matter. "No. Everything's happening so quick, is all."

She laughed, giving his knee a pat before rearing back in her chair. "Life in the fast lane. Hold onto your hat, cowboy, and prepare yourself for a hell of a ride."

Sighing, Cody stood, reaching for her hand. "You better prepare yourself for a ride. We've got that cow and calf to move, remember?"

Minutes later, Cody swung up in the saddle and turned his horse toward the cow and calf who stood nervously in the paddock outside the barn. "Open the gate," he called out. "I'll start 'em out."

With a quick nod, Reggie leaned down from her horse to unlatch the gate and swing it wide. Backing Cupid out of the way, she waited while Cody herded the cow and calf out into the pasture, then reined her horse alongside his.

"Let's keep 'em close to the fence. I don't want to take a chance of them trying to join this herd of steers."

"Okay, boss."

At the tag, Cody snapped his head around to frown at her.

She grinned, lifting her shoulder in a shrug. "Every trail drive has a trail boss. I bow to your age and experience."

Chuckling, Cody clicked his horse into a trot. "It'll be the first time."

Still pumped from her conversation with Benning, Reggie let the jab roll right off her without comment. She tipped her face to the sun, letting its rays warm her. "Isn't this glorious?" she murmured appreciatively. "I wonder sometimes how I could have left it all."

Cody lifted his chin, taking in the expanse of blue sky, the puffy white clouds that hung overhead. "Yeah, it's a sight all right. Personally, I can't imagine living anywhere else."

"You did, though, for a while," she reminded him.

He turned to look at her. "While I was on the circuit?"

At her nod, he chuckled again. "If you count living out of a truck, living, I guess I did. But that was only temporary. I always knew I'd be coming back."

Reggie looked at him in surprise. "You did?"

"Well, sure. I only left to drum up enough money to start a place of my own."

"I never knew that," she said in genuine surprise.

"I thought you left because—" She started to say she thought he left to put distance between himself and her, but she couldn't make herself form the words. Eleven years later, they still hurt. "—because you wanted out of Temptation," she said instead.

"Hell, no! I love it here. Temptation's the only home I've ever known."

"How can you be sure there isn't some place that you would like even better? I mean, after all, you've never lived anywhere else."

Cody pondered that a moment as he kept a watchful eye on the cow and calf. "It's kind of like a relationship between a man and a woman," he said thoughtfully. "There's always another woman up the road just like there's always another town, but if you're always chasin', you can't appreciate and enjoy the one you've already found."

Though the example was offered to explain his feelings about Temptation, Reggie found herself focusing on the man-woman relationship he used. "You've never married," she said, studying him.

"No. But you did."

Reggie heard the accusation in his voice. "Yes, but it was a mistake," she replied. "I should have never married Kevin."

Cody twisted his head around to peer at her. "Then why did you?"

"Loneliness, I guess." Reggie felt heat crawl up her neck as she realized how foolish that sounded. "When I first moved to Houston, I was so homesick I thought I'd die. I met Kevin in a real estate class I was taking at the university. He had just moved to Houston, too, and didn't know anyone." She lifted her shoulder in a self-conscious shrug. "We started dating."

Cody tore his gaze away, his lips thinned to a tight line, not wanting to think of Regan with another man. He lifted a hand, pointing ahead to the cow. "She's drifting. Nose her back toward the fence."

Thinking he wanted to end the conversation, Reggie did as instructed but when she returned to ride alongside Cody, he picked up the conversation right where she'd left off.

"So you married him? After knowing him less than six months?"

That he knew when she married Kevin surprised Reggie. "How did you know I'd only known him six months?"

It was Cody's turn to be embarrassed. "'Cause I went to Houston to track you down." He narrowed an eye at the pasture ahead. "Court records are open to the public."

Reggie reined her horse to a stop and grabbed Cody's arm, forcing him to stop beside her. "You followed me?"

One side of his mouth twisted into a frown. "Not right away. Harley seemed to think we'd be better off leaving you alone. I disagreed."

"But why didn't you contact me?"

Cody snorted. "What good would it have done? You were already married." Shifting his gaze ahead, he quickly changed the subject. "I'll work my way around the cow and open the gate. You just keep pushing 'em on."

Reggie stared after him, stunned by what she'd just learned. *He'd come after her and she'd never known!*

"Cody! Wait!"

Cody wheeled his horse back around after sending the cow and calf past the gate, his mouth curled in a scowl. "What?"

She urged Cupid up alongside his horse and placed a hand on his arm. "Thank you," she said softly. "You'll never know how much it means to know that you tried to find me."

Cody sighed, unable to hold on to the anger. Not with her looking at him that way. Besides, it was all in the past. It wouldn't do any good to resurrect it all now. "You're welcome."

He leaned over, looping an arm around her waist. Reggie squealed as he dragged her from the back of her horse and settled her on the saddle in front of him. Spooked, Cupid took off at a run while Cody struggled to keep his own horse from following.

Slinging an arm around Cody's neck to keep from falling, Reggie cried, "What in the world are you doing?"

Cody grinned. "Ever heard of the mile high club?"

Cocking her head, Reggie frowned at him. "I think that's reserved for airplanes."

Cody lifted a shoulder and clicked to the horse, sending him into a lope. "When I ride, I always feel like I'm flying."

Seven

"Where to first?" Cody asked as he slipped behind the steering wheel of his truck later that day.

Reggie pursed her lips thoughtfully. "We'll want something close to town, but far enough out so that the plant doesn't create an eyesore."

"There's the Murreys' place, Roy and Thelma. Probably more land than you need, but I heard they're wanting to sell out and retire."

"How much land?"

"Oh, about seventy-five acres, I'd guess."

"That leaves plenty of room for expansion," she murmured, mulling it over. "What else is available?"

"Well, the Coopers' old farm is still vacant. When they passed on, they left it to some distant relative who lives somewhere up in Missouri I think, but the folks have never done anything with their inheritance, other than pay the taxes on it."

"I remember that place," Reggie said, her eyes sharpening in interest. "About two miles west of town. They raised laying hens, didn't they?"

"Yeah. Ruth was fit to be tied when she realized that she'd have to find somebody new to supply her with eggs for the store."

Reggie laughed, imagining Ruth grousing over the inconvenience. "I'll bet she was. Let's check out the Cooper place first."

With a nod, Cody shifted into gear and headed out. They drove in silence, with her sitting beside him, her hand resting familiarly on his knee. They passed the high school where an assortment of cars lined the street. Reggie twisted her head around, peering at her old alma mater as they drove past.

"I can't believe they were going to close Temptation High," she murmured.

Cody firmed his lips. "Yeah, it would've been a shame all right. The only thing that's kept it open this long is the fact that two of the smaller towns nearby had to close their schools and they sent their students over here."

Reggie sighed, squeezing his thigh. "Benning will move here," she promised. "And when he does, we won't have to worry about closing any schools. He'll bring families here with kids enough to fill all Temptation's schools."

Cody ducked his head to peer at her. "You really think you can pull this off?"

Reggie gave her chin a determined bob. "You're damned right I can. It's just a matter of putting all the pieces together."

"And you've got all the pieces?"

"I've got Benning, and if this property is as good as I remember it, we'll have another piece of the puzzle. Then it's just a matter of working out the housing needs with that developer Will told me about. And then convincing Benning that Temptation's the place for him."

Cody just shook his head. "If anybody can do it, you can."

Reggie smiled, pleased by the compliment. "Don't worry about Benning. I can handle him."

After showing Reggie the Cooper property, Cody drove her back out to the ranch and left her there while he ran back to town to locate the name and address of the Coopers' relatives.

With only hours left before Harley and Mary Claire returned from their honeymoon, Reggie decided she'd put off as long as she could going through the things Harley had stored for her in the attic.

Unsure what memories awaited her, she climbed the familiar staircase, remembering other times she'd made the trip with her mother. They'd spent many a rainy day in the attic, going through the old trunk which her mother had referred to as her memory box. With her mother's help, Reggie had tried on her mother's wedding veil, laughed over old photos and cried at memories each drew.

The wooden steps creaked beneath her weight, just as they always had done, and the banister still wobbled just a little in her hand. Taking a deep breath, she pushed open the door that led to the attic she hadn't had the courage to face since her mother's death.

Sunlight streamed through the four dormer windows, turning to silver the cobwebs that hung from every corner. Cloths draped ghost-like shapes, probably furniture stored there for years. Curious, she lifted the corner of one cloth and sucked in a shocked breath. *Mother's writing desk!* she cried silently. She'd thought the piece lost forever when Susan had redecorated the house after marrying Harley.

Quickly, she threw back the cloth, fully exposing the mahogany table her mother had cherished so much. Smoothing a hand across the burled wood top, she fought back tears, wondering how Harley had managed to save it.

Anxious to see what else lay beneath the dust covers, she raced around the room, throwing back cloths, sending dust to thicken the air. The cherry table and eight chairs that had graced the dining room. The matching buffet. The antique sideboard that her mother had lovingly refinished for the breakfast room when she had first married Harley's father.

Reggie placed a hand against her thudding heart. So many pieces were missing, but that Harley had managed to save any of them from Susan's vicious hand was unbelievable.

Seeing a smaller, odd-shaped piece in a far corner, she crossed to it and threw back the cloth. The round-topped steamer trunk where her mother had kept her treasures. Her wedding gown. Reggie's christening dress. Pictures of her first husband, Reggie's father. Albums filled with pictures and mementos of Reggie's first years.

Not daring to hope, she carefully lifted the lid. The smell of smoke and charred paper assailed her nose.

Her stomach pitched and her head swam as memories pressed down on her. Bracing a hand against the trunk, she sank to the floor, envisioning again the day she'd found Susan in front of the fireplace in the den, the trunk at her side. While Reggie had watched in sick horror, Susan had fed the memories of Reggie's life to the greedy flames.

Harley had heard her scream and come running. But not in time. Susan had accomplished what she'd set out to do…she'd stolen from Reggie the few physical memories she had left of her mother and father. Reggie had run, just as she always had when caught in a confrontation with her sister-in-law, seeking solace in the hayloft in the barn. Cody had found her there, sobbing her heart out, and had offered comfort as he had so many times in the past.

It was that night that they'd first made love. In his arms she'd received love and understanding, a comfort that helped ease the loss of so much. Seeing him as her knight in shining armor, her means of escape, Reggie had begged him to run away with her and marry her. But Cody had only added to her anguish by refusing her.

Pushing back the painful memory, Reggie rose to her knees to peer inside the trunk. Carefully gathering in her hands some of the trunk's contents, she sank back on her heels, spreading the charred pieces on the floor in front of her. She picked up a piece of fabric, yellowed with age and burned around the edges. Her christening dress, she realized, recognizing the scrap of hand-embroidered linen. Tears spurting to her eyes, she clutched the piece of fabric to her breasts. Harley hadn't been able to save the dress itself, but he'd managed to salvage a piece of it for her.

Still holding the fabric against her heart, she reached for a blackened photo. Though curled from the heat of the fire, she could make out the faces of her mother and father. Dressed in a wedding gown she'd sewn herself, her mother, radiant on her wedding day, smiled up at her new husband. Reggie remembered her mother showing the photo to her. Though she'd lost her husband to death and had remarried several years later, Reggie's mother had always kept his memory alive for Reggie by showing her pictures and telling her stories of a father she didn't remember.

Sighing, she laid it aside and picked up another.

Cody stood at the top of the stairway, looking at Regan sitting on the floor, surrounded by charred reminders of her past, unsure whether he should intrude on this private moment.

But then he heard the first sob rack her body and knew he couldn't leave her to face this alone. Quickly crossing the wood-planked floor, he hunkered down behind her, catching her shoulders in his hands.

"Regan, honey," he soothed.

She twisted around, burying her face against his chest. "Oh, Cody," she cried. "It's so unfair."

"I know," he murmured, rubbing a hand down her spine. "I know."

"Why did she hate me so much that she would do this to me?" she sobbed.

He heaved a sigh. "Because she was jealous, I suppose."

"Of what?"

"Your relationship with Harley. Susan didn't like to share and she was forced to share not only Harley, but this house with you."

"But she was his wife! She belonged here. I was just his stepsister. How could she be jealous of me?"

Cody just shook his head, thinking of all the conversations he'd had with Harley on this same subject over the years. Poor Harley had been trapped in the difficult position of having to keep the peace between his wife and his stepsister, a no-win situation, no matter which way he approached it. Though Harley was fully aware that the problems between the two were all created by Susan, he'd tried not to take sides and had done his best to keep his family together.

The arguments between Susan and Harley that took place after Regan ran away had finally put the skids on a marriage already doomed for failure. In the end, Harley had lost them all—his stepsister, his wife and children. It was only when Mary Claire came along that he began to heal.

"I wish I knew," Cody murmured. "Susan had problems that stretched way beyond her relationship with you. She just chose you as her target."

A shudder passed through her and she withdrew from his arms. "It's still funny, isn't it?" she said as she wiped her fingertips beneath her eyes. "That if I'd stuck it out, I would never have had to leave?"

"No, I guess you wouldn't have," Cody murmured, thinking of all of the twists of fate that had brought them to this point. Looking at Regan, he wondered how things would have turned out for them if she'd stayed. "Regan," he began.

A sound outside had her scrambling to her feet. She

ran to the dormer window and looked out. "Oh, my gosh! They're here!" she cried as she spotted Harley and Mary Claire stepping from their car. She whirled, turning her horrified gaze on Cody. "I can't let them see me like this. Would you mind intercepting them while I run to my room and patch up my makeup?"

Cody pushed to his feet. "No, I don't mind."

Her composure regained and her makeup touched up, Reggie served coffee to the returning honeymooners. "So, how was Cozumel?"

Mary Claire sighed dramatically as she plopped down in a chair at the kitchen table beside her husband. "Paradise. It took Harley about two days to relax and quit worrying about the ranch, but after that we had a marvelous time. We went snorkeling, chartered a boat with Leighanna and Hank and went deep-sea fishing and spent the rest of the time soaking up the sun and just relaxing." She lifted her face, smiling as Reggie placed a cup of coffee in front of her. "You'll never know how much we appreciate the trip and your willingness to stay and watch the kids. I can hardly wait for them to get home from school."

Reggie slipped into a chair beside Cody and reached beneath the table to lace her fingers with his on his thigh. "It was my pleasure."

Harley lifted his cup to Cody in a salute. "And you, too, buddy. We couldn't have gone if you hadn't agreed to look after the place."

Cody just shook his head as he rubbed Regan's knuckles down his thigh, knowing he should be thanking Harley instead of the other way around. If Harley hadn't given him the responsibility of the livestock, he wouldn't have had the opportunity to spend so much time with Regan. "No thanks needed."

Harley turned his gaze to his stepsister. "How much longer can you stay?"

Cody stiffened at the question, not wanting to hear Regan's reply. They'd avoided the subject, though both knew their time together was drawing to an end.

"I guess I'll leave tomorrow, after you two have had a chance to settle back in. I really need to get back to work, although I did manage to get some work done here." She smiled sheepishly at her brother. "I sort of commandeered your office. Sorry I didn't ask first."

Harley waved away her apology. "Heck, it's as much your office as mine. In fact—" He rose, pushing out of his chair. "There's a little business we need to discuss. Now's as good a time as any."

He returned minutes later, carrying a thick ledger and a folder brimming with paper. He set the folder on the table. "These are all your bank statements over the past ten years."

Reggie looked at him in confusion. "But I closed out my account before I moved."

Harley dropped into the seat opposite hers, his attention focused on the ledger in his hands. "I opened you another one to put in your share of the ranch's profits."

Reggie's mouth dropped open. "But, Harley! The ranch is yours!"

He shook his head. "No. When Dad died, he left the place to both of us. I've just been managing your share in your absence. Now that you're back—or rather now that I know where you are—you can take a more active role in your inheritance."

He laid the ledger in front of her. "Here are our books." He flipped several pages. "And here is our current worth."

She shoved the book back across the table after just a cursory look, but not before Cody caught a glimpse of the amount at the bottom of the page. He hadn't meant to look, but the figures were there right in front of him. The size of the number didn't surprise him, he had a pretty good idea of the value of the Kerr ranch, he just hadn't known that Regan owned half. He felt that gap that stretched between them widen even more.

"It's not *ours*, Harley," Reggie argued. "It's *yours*. You're the one who stayed and worked the place." She shook her head, rearing back in her chair, as if by doing so she could distance herself from Harley's offer. "I have my own business, my own investments. I don't need any part of the ranch. Besides, I can't accept something that isn't rightfully mine."

"But it is yours," he insisted. "Dad left it to both of us."

Seeing that her refusal was hurting him, Reggie reached across the table to lay her hand on his. "Then I'm giving you my share. The only thing I ever wanted from my stepfather was his love and he gave me that generously while he was alive. The ranch is yours, as it should be. I'll have my lawyer draw up whatever papers are necessary to transfer my share of the money and the land back to you." She plopped back against her chair, putting an end to the conversation. "Enough of that. I think we need to plan a little welcome home party for you all." She turned to Cody. "Can I count on you to man the grill?"

If Cody had doubted her plans to leave Temptation, he didn't any longer. She was going back. Even after being offered financial security right here in Temptation, she was still going back to Houston. Numbed by that knowledge, Cody slowly nodded his head. "Yeah, sure."

"I'll call Hank and Leighanna and see if they can join us," Reggie continued, always ready to take charge. "We'll cook steaks and corn on the cob out on the grill and I'll bake potatoes in the oven." She turned to Mary Claire. "Are you up to making some of your famous baked beans?"

Reggie picked up her plate from the patio table and reached for Mary Claire's.

"Oh, no you don't," Mary Claire warned, brushing Reggie's hand from her plate. "You and Cody did all the cooking. The rest of us can do kitchen duty."

"But—"

"No buts," Harley said and took her plate from her. "Come on, Hank," he ordered. "Get off your lazy butt. I've got an apron in the kitchen with your name on it."

Grumbling, Hank followed Harley and Mary Claire into the house, helped along with gentle prods from Leighanna who followed behind.

Left alone with Cody, Reggie didn't know quite what to say. He'd been unusually quiet during dinner. She'd noticed it, wondering if he was feeling the same apprehension as she, knowing that tomorrow she would be leaving.

"Let's go for a ride, Cody," she suggested, hoping that the distraction would draw him from his dark mood.

Nodding his agreement, he caught up his hat from the seat of the swing, and led Reggie to his truck.

He negotiated the drive in silence, but at the end of the long road that connected the Kerr ranch to the highway, he stopped and turned to her. "Where do you want to go?"

She sighed, pressing her shoulder against his as she stared out into the darkness beyond the windshield. "The old hunting cabin," she murmured. "Where you used to live."

Cody started to suggest another destination, anywhere but there, but couldn't think of another place to take her. Temptation didn't have a whole lot to offer, a fact that was beginning to rub him a little raw. With a shrug, he turned right, onto the highway.

Regan laid her head on his shoulder, a hand on his thigh, as they drove through the night. Moonlight added its own illumination to that of the truck's headlights as Cody reached the end of the highway and made the turn between the familiar gap in the fencing that led to the cabin.

Unlike the last time he'd made this trip, he drove slowly, maneuvering his truck carefully down the deeply rutted road. When the site where the cabin had once stood came into view, he veered off the path, stopping in front of the pile of debris.

She lifted her head from his shoulder and leaned forward to stare through the windshield, her mouth open, her fingers digging into his thigh. "Oh, Cody," she cried. "It's gone."

Ashamed to admit that he was the one who'd leveled it, Cody lifted a shoulder. "The place was vacant for years. Nothing but rats lived there since I moved out."

"But it was your home," she moaned pitifully, feeling the loss for him.

Cody snorted. "That place was never home to me. It was just a place to stay."

Reggie looked at him then, hearing the bitterness in his reply and wondered if his quarters behind the sheriff's house was that too, just a place to stay. She turned, angling on the seat until she faced him fully. "Have you ever considered building here?" she asked softly.

Cody turned his face to the windshield, looking out, remembering his plan of making it big on the circuit and coming back to Temptation and buying a place for himself and Regan. "No, not here."

"Where, then?"

"When I left, I always planned to come back and buy some land of my own and build there. Where didn't matter. So long as it was in Temptation."

"Why didn't you?"

He had to give himself a hard shake to pull himself from the memories. "I don't know," he said turning to her, knowing full well that the reason he'd never bought a bigger spread of land was because Regan hadn't been there to share it with him. But he wouldn't tell her that, not now when she was preparing to leave again. "Didn't seem important anymore, I guess."

Not wanting to dwell on the thought of her leaving, he pressed his back against the door and propped a foot on the seat beside her. Taking her hand, he tugged her around until her back rested against his chest and her head in the crook of his shoulder. He stretched out his legs, twining them with hers, and wrapped his arms around her waist. Needing to have her as close as humanly possible, he snugged her tight against his chest and buried his nose in her hair.

Sighing, she lifted a hand to his cheek, her gaze fixed on the stars that hung overhead. "I'm going to miss you, Cody."

A wad of emotion rose to clog Cody's throat. "I'm going to miss you, too," he murmured.

"Will you come to see me?" she asked, trying to hide the uncertainty in her voice.

When he didn't reply, she turned in his arms, looking up at him. She saw the answer in his eyes. "You won't, will you?" she whispered, her heart breaking.

When still he didn't answer, she drew in a ragged breath. "So this is it, huh?" she asked, fighting back tears.

"Regan, I—"

She pressed a finger to his lips, not wanting to hear his reasons. "No. Don't, please." She turned fully, drawing to her knees. "Make love to me, Cody," she whispered as she dipped her face to his. "Love me one last time."

On a groan, he pulled her to him, taking her mouth and crushing it against his. He didn't want her to go, couldn't ask her to stay, but he could give her this. He could make love to her one last time.

But he'd take it slow, he told himself. He'd give them both memories enough to last a lifetime. Softening the kiss, he caught her lower lip between his teeth and nipped lightly. "Let's move outside," he murmured. "Under the stars."

Willing to go with him anywhere, she shifted away, untangling her legs from his, then climbed down from the truck after him. Cody grabbed a blanket from behind the seat, then gathered her hand in his, leading her across the field to a small rise that seemed to swell from the ground in a perfect circle, an altar reaching for the star-studded sky.

With her help, he spread the blanket across the tall grass, matting it into a soft bed for them, then took her hand, turning her to face him. With the moonlight guiding his movements and the stars winking their approval, he dropped his hands to her silk blouse and worked the buttons free. Gently he lifted the blouse over her shoulders and slowly drew it down her arms, then unhooked her bra and let it drop between them.

He didn't have any words to offer her, didn't trust himself to even try to form the words he wanted so badly to say, but chose instead to let his hands express his feelings. Gently, he placed them on her shoulders and let the tips of his fingers drift slowly downward, shaping the gentle swell of her breasts, then he drew them upward to the valley between. Heat raced through her. He felt it through his fingertips pressed against her bare flesh, saw it in the passion that glazed her eyes. With his gaze on hers, he laid a palm over her heart.

He felt its quickening beat, felt the heat of her skin blend with his. Regan. His Regan. How would he ever be able to let her go?

Not now, he told himself, forcing the thought away. He wouldn't think about tomorrow, only tonight. On a sigh, he dipped his face over hers, needing to lose himself in her taste. Their lips touched briefly, drew apart, then touched again, each seeking, tasting, testing. He felt her arms slide between them, felt her fingers tug at the buttons on his shirt, but he only had thoughts for the taste of her, the feel of her hot, sensual mouth beneath his.

He would remember this time, he promised himself, as a gift that he never expected, without the regrets that had haunted him in the past. For Regan was his, if only for this moment, and he wouldn't look beyond the now.

Her hands flattened against his chest, smoothing upward to push his shirt over his shoulders. Cool air hit his back, pebbling his skin as the shirt dropped away, then her hands, hot and demanding, were there, digging into his flesh to force him nearer, warming him with her heat.

Impatient. Regan had always been impatient. Unwilling to wait, always ready to hustle things along to meet some internal clock of her own. It had been so eleven years ago the first time they'd made love, and it had been so when she'd asked him to run away with her and marry her.

But Cody wouldn't allow her to rush. Not this time. Not now when this memory was all he'd have once she was gone.

Taking her elbows, he took a step back, dragging his mouth from hers. Unsteady, she braced her hands on his arms and lifted her gaze to his. In her eyes, he saw the questions that pushed their way through the layers of passion. But he didn't have any answers for her, only a need that was speeding quickly out of control.

Toeing off his boots, he dropped his hands to his belt buckle and stripped out of his jeans. Regan mimicked his movements, kicking free of her shoes, peeling off her slacks. When she straightened, she stood before him, gloriously naked, with the moon behind her painting her smooth skin with its angel-soft light.

Cody sucked in a breath at the sight of her and had to remind himself of the need to go slow. But then her scent drifted to him in the night air, that womanly, seductive scent that he knew he'd always remember, and he felt his resolve give way to raw need. Taking her hand, he guided her down to the blanket then wadded his jeans behind her head for a pillow. Stretching out beside her, he laid his palm across her stomach. Nerves jumped to life beneath her skin at his touch.

"You're so beautiful, Regan. So, so beautiful."

Tears spurted to her eyes. "Oh, Cody," she murmured, reaching out to draw his face to hers.

He took her mouth with his, claiming what he could of her, needing to possess her if only for one night. The heat was there, the acceptance, as he tongued her mouth open. Sweet, oh so sweet, he thought as he skimmed his tongue across her teeth. He was sure the taste of her would haunt him always.

He slipped his hand lower on her abdomen to cup her femininity. She moaned, shifting, offering herself to him. Dipping his fingers between her legs, he teased her. Soft, slick, she flowered for him.

Her mouth grew hot and demanding against his, her lips burning as her tongue tangled with his in a silent mating...and Cody lost the fingertip grip he'd held on his control.

He hauled her on top of him, holding her mouth against his, and settled her hips against his groin. Heat from their joined bodies flamed, threatening to consume them as he cupped his hands on her buttocks and guided her over him.

She tore her mouth from his at the first thrust and planted her hands against his chest. Groaning her pleasure, she arched, her head lolling back. Moonlight spilled across her face, and Cody knew he'd never seen a more glorious sight than Regan caught in the throes of passion.

They raced through the night, each seeking that elusive fulfillment, wanting it and yet holding off, for each knew that this would be their last time.

Cody felt the tension build in her, felt her fingers curl against his chest, her thighs tighten against his hips. He reached for her, bringing himself up to meet her.

"Now, Regan," he growled, taking her mouth with his. "Now!"

She fought him, wanting to hang on a moment longer, to cling to these feelings for as long as she could. But her body defied her, rising to meet Cody's challenge. Crying out, she sank her nails into his chest, clinging to him as her body exploded around him.

He held her pressed tight against him as the shudders quaked through her, as the muscles slowly relaxed, until, breathless, she dropped her forehead to his shoulder on a sigh.

"I love you, Cody," she whispered against his damp skin.

A lump rose to close Cody's throat. And he loved her, but what good did love do them when there was so much standing between them?

"I know, Reggie," he murmured, cupping the back of her head tenderly in his hand. "And I love you."

She waited, holding her breath, willing him with all her heart to carry that declaration one step further…to ask her to stay in Temptation with him. But though he continued to hold her, his palms smoothing up and down her spine, his heart touching and warming hers in the cool night air, he remained silent.

Biting back tears, Reggie tightened her arms around him, knowing that she couldn't be the one to ask. Not this time. Her pride simply wouldn't allow it.

Reggie took one last glance at her reflection, and frowned at her puffy red eyes. "What do you expect after a sleepless night?" she muttered, as she turned away from the mirror.

Grabbing her bag, she quickly strode through the house and out the kitchen door to the patio where everyone had gathered. Mary Claire, Harley, Stephie, Jimmy, Leighanna and Hank.

But not Cody.

She caught herself before the tears came again. She knew he wouldn't come to say goodbye to her. They'd said their goodbyes the night before.

"Well, I'm off!" she called out gaily, forcing a bright smile to her face.

Harley took her bag from her hand and slung an

arm around her shoulder as he walked with her to her car. "Don't be a stranger, hear?"

Blinking back tears, she pressed the trunk release on her key ring. "I won't, I promise." She stepped back while Harley stored her bag in the trunk then slammed it shut. "And y'all have to promise to come see me, too. Okay?" she asked, turning to include them all in the invitation.

Mary Claire caught the hem of her apron to dab at her eyes. "We will," she promised, trying her best not to cry.

Leighanna covered her face with her hands, giving in to the tears. Hank pulled her against him, shooting a wink at Reggie as he sought to soothe. "Instead of blubbering 'cause she's leaving, Leighanna, why don't you tell Reggie our news."

Leighanna turned her face against his shoulder, her sobs increasing. "Y-you tell h-her," she sobbed. "I—I can't."

"There, there," Hank soothed, dipping his head over hers to drop a kiss on the top of her head. He glanced up, his face splitting in a wide smile. "We're gonna have a baby," he announced proudly.

Reggie's mouth dropped open. "A baby!"

Hank's chest swelled. "Yep. A baby." He chuckled, hugging Leighanna against his side. "We got a little head start on the honeymoon. The baby's due in about eight months."

"A baby," Reggie repeated dully, then shouted, "A baby!" as the news finally sank in. She raced across the patio and wrapped her arms around them both. "I'm so happy for you," she cried, her tears blending with Leighanna's as she pressed her cheek to hers. Leighanna sobbed all the more.

"Leighanna's happy, too," Hank said, grinning at Reagan over the top of his wife's head. "She's just having a little trouble with these roller-coaster hormones right now. You know how these pregnant women are."

No, she didn't know, but that didn't dampen Reggie's excitement any. She drew away a step, taking Leighanna's hand in hers. "You take care of yourself, all right?"

Leighanna pressed a knuckle beneath her nose and nodded, still unable to speak.

Reggie shifted her gaze to Hank's. "And I'm depending on you to make sure that she does."

Hank saluted smartly. "Yes, sir, ma'am!"

Reggie laughed, then turned to Jimmy and Stephie. "Okay, you two. Give your Aunt Reggie a hug."

Stephie ran to throw her arms around Reggie's waist, but Jimmy hung back, dragging the tip of a tennis shoe in the dirt.

"Thanks for staying with us, Aunt Reggie."

Reggie dropped to her knees in front of Stephie. "You're welcome, squirt." She gave her a quick kiss, then turned to Jimmy. Knowing that he wasn't going to put up with any public displays of affection, she ruffled his hair. "Now I expect you to look after that calf and call me with reports at least once a week."

Jimmy glanced up, obviously relieved that he wasn't going to have to suffer through a hug. "Okay," he mumbled, trying not to smile.

With a ragged sigh, Reggie turned to Mary Claire, anxious to get away before she shamed herself with more tears. "Take care of my big brother," she whispered as she gave her new sister-in-law a quick hug.

"I will."

Releasing Mary Claire, she turned to Harley. "See ya, bro."

Harley scooped her up and planted a kiss smack on her lips, just as he had when she was younger, before setting her back on the ground. "See ya, sis."

Fighting tears, Reggie turned for her car.

Harley shifted his gaze to the drive behind her, frowning. "I'd've thought Cody would come by to see you off."

Reggie paused with one hand on the door and looked back. "We said our goodbyes last night." With a last wave, she ducked into the car and started the engine.

Then, and only then, did she let the tears fall.

Eight

The days crawled by for Cody, one stacking up on top of the other until almost three weeks had passed since Regan had left town. He tried not to think about her, tried to focus instead on his job and on the newcomers who continued to trickle into Temptation.

Sometimes he'd almost succeed at the task, but only for a minute or two. Then something would bring her to mind again, some silly little something like the scent of the wind, the way the sun struck a roof of tin turning it to silver, the way the sunflowers tipped their faces to the sun as if cherishing its warmth and light just as she had done so many times during the week she'd spent there.

He couldn't explain it, didn't even try, but he would just find his thoughts drifting to her again.

In need of something to take his mind off Regan,

he tried to think of somewhere he could go, something he could do that wouldn't bring her to mind. He immediately ruled out the Kerr ranch. There were too many memories there to haunt him. His frustration grew when he realized there wasn't a place in town that *didn't* draw some memory.

The End of the Road, he thought. It was the one place in Temptation where he'd never taken Regan, and that was only because it had been closed the week she was in town. Whipping his truck around, he headed for Hank's bar.

He turned onto the parking lot, his tires spitting gravel behind him and braked to a stop by the front entrance. With a sigh, he climbed down. Shoving his hat onto the back of his head, he opened the screen door and stepped inside, letting the door slam shut behind him.

Hank glanced up from his spot behind the bar.

"Hey, Cody!" he called. "How about a cold one?"

Cody slipped onto a bar stool, and pulled off his hat, raking his fingers through his hair. "Sounds good. Where's Leighanna?"

"Gone to Austin, shopping with Mary Claire." Hank shook his head, chuckling as he stuck a mug under the tap. "Don't know where we're going to put the stuff she's already bought for the baby, much less the baby itself when it comes." He shoved the mug across the scarred surface toward Cody, then leaned, folding his arms across the bar. "Guess I'm going to have to break down and lease Mary Claire's house from her, just so I can have some room to move around."

Cody lifted a shoulder, then let it drop as if even that much movement required more energy than he had. "You could do worse."

Hank eyed him, wondering about Cody's mood. He hadn't seen much of his friend since Regan had left town. In fact, he hadn't seen him at all, except in passing. Just that morning Leighanna had made a comment about his absence, speculating that he was nursing a lovesick heart. Hank had brushed off the remark, sure that Leighanna was wrong. But now he wondered....

"Yeah, I guess I could," he murmured. On impulse, he grabbed a mug for himself. "So what brings you to the End of the Road? Haven't seen much of you lately."

Again, Cody lifted a shoulder, staring at his beer, not wanting to admit his real reason for dropping by. "Just needed something cold to drink, is all."

The front door squeaked open again, then slammed shut. Hank lifted his gaze. "Well, I'll be durned," he called out as Harley stepped inside. "Not often that I have the chance to share a beer with my two best friends." He reached for another mug and filled it, then placed it on the bar.

Harley slid onto the stool next to Cody and reached for the offered beer on a weary sigh. "Man, am I dry. I've been riding fence all morning." He took a sip, angling slightly to glance at Cody. "What brings you to the End of the Road this time of day?"

Cody scowled. "Can't a man even stop in for a beer without instigating a public inquest?"

Harley arched one eyebrow at the anger in Cody's

reply. "Sure," he said and glanced at Hank. "It's just that we haven't seen much of you lately."

Almost Hank's exact words, Cody thought in growing frustration. "I've been busy," he muttered.

Harley and Hank shared a knowing glance. Both had suffered the strain of a lovesick heart and recognized the signs immediately.

"Have you heard from Regan?" Harley asked.

"No. Was I supposed to?"

Harley lifted a shoulder. "No, just thought she might have called to give you an update on that Benning deal she's so fired up about."

"Well, she hasn't."

Shifting his gaze between the two men, Hank decided Harley might need a little help. "Looked to me like you two might have stirred something up while we were out of town."

Cody slammed his mug down onto the bar and shot Hank a killing look. "You know, that's what I hate most about Temptation. Everyone's always sticking their nose in everybody else's business."

Hank lifted his hands and took a step back. "Hey! I was just making an innocent observation. No cause to get your dander up."

Grimacing, Cody lifted his beer again and took a long drink.

Harley shifted on his seat. "Regan's due in town this weekend to introduce Benning to the mayor and show him that land y'all looked at. Mary Claire's decided to throw a party. She told me to pass the word."

With a cautious glance Cody's way, Hank stepped back up to the bar. "What's the occasion?"

"Regan's birthday."

Cody stiffened, then forced himself to relax, muscle by muscle.

Harley noticed the reaction but decided it might not be wise to comment on it. "Yeah, my little sister's going to be turning twenty-eight. Mary Claire thought it would be fun to throw a surprise party in her honor. Just a small affair, mostly family, but since we consider you guys family, you're all invited."

"You can count on us," Hank promised, clinking his mug against Harley's.

"What about you, Cody?" Harley asked, turning to him.

Cody tipped his mug, staring miserably at his beer. And he'd thought he could escape thoughts of Regan by stopping in at the End of the Road. What a joke! Now here he sat, a formal invitation to see her again being shoved in his face. He didn't want to see Regan again. Saying goodbye the last time had been hard enough. Confronting her again would only remind him of all he'd lost, what he couldn't have.

"I'll see," he mumbled noncommittally before lifting his mug and draining it.

Cody sat reared back in his chair, his hands folded behind his head, staring out the front window. He told himself he wasn't watching for Regan's arrival, but he knew it was a lie. The mayor had told him when she was expected to arrive, and though he knew he was only torturing himself, he watched and waited, hoping for a glimpse of her.

Right on time, the Lexus streaked past the front window of his office and whipped into a space in front of the mayor's office two doors down. A sleek

black Jaguar followed. He watched as Regan stepped
from her car, smiling across the padded sunroof at the
man who climbed from the Jaguar.

Benning?

Cody straightened, pulling his hands from behind
his head to stare. The man didn't look anything like
Cody had expected. For some reason, he'd envisioned
an older man, bald-headed, pot-bellied, with a thick
cigar clamped between his teeth.

This guy could've stepped straight off the cover of
GQ. From the top of his razor-cut hair to the tips of
his Italian loafers, he exuded both youth and wealth
as he returned Regan's smile. Cody watched the
man's lips move and wondered what he said that had
Regan laughing so gaily as she crossed to the front
of the car to meet him.

While Cody watched like some kind of sick voy-
eur, Benning offered his arm. Smiling up at him, Regan slipped her hand around the bend in his elbow
and walked with him into the mayor's office.

Cody tore his gaze away from the sight, his gut
clenching in reaction. Jealousy. He recognized the
emotion and knew he had no right to feel it, but in
spite of that fact, he felt it slip its bony green fingers
around his heart and squeeze.

That was the kind of man Regan deserved, he told
himself, the kind of man who'd fit the lifestyle she'd
created for herself since leaving Temptation. She
didn't need him. Cody Fipes was nothing but a broken-down cowboy, serving time as sheriff in what
must be to Regan a two-bit town. But no matter how
hard he tried, he couldn't make the jealousy go away.

The phone rang and Cody snatched up the receiver. "Sheriff's office," he barked angrily.

"Hey, Cody, Mayor Acres here."

Cody caught the bridge of his nose between thumb and index finger and squeezed, sure that he knew what was coming. "Yeah, what can I do for you, Mayor?"

"Regan's just arrived. I want you to come over so I can introduce you to Cal Benning, Regan's client from Houston."

Client? After what Cody had just witnessed, he wondered if Cal might be more than just a client. "Is it necessary?" he asked. "I'm pretty busy."

"Won't take a minute," the mayor assured him pleasantly, but Cody heard the order beneath the response.

Knowing he didn't have a choice in the matter, Cody muttered, "I'll be right there." Slamming down the receiver, he pushed away from his desk. He stopped by the door to pull his hat from the peg and then rammed it onto his head. Jerking open the door, he strode down the sidewalk, quickly closing the distance that stretched between his office and the mayor's. With a scowling glance at Regan's car, he opened the door to the mayor's office and stepped inside, dragging off his hat.

Seated in front of Acres's desk, Regan rose, as did Cal, at his entrance and turned to greet him. Cody felt his breath back up into his lungs at the sight of her. Dressed in trousers and a tunic jacket the color of aged whiskey, she looked every inch the successful businesswoman. Her hair was swept up in some kind of fancy twist and he had the strongest urge to rip the pins out and let down her hair. He wanted his Regan. The familiar one. Not this citified woman who faced him now.

"Hello, Cody," she said, extending her hand.

Cody shifted his hat to his left hand and took hers in his right, resenting the formality of her greeting. The feel of her satin-soft skin against his callused one, the warmth of her amber eyes, drew memories he didn't even want to think about. "Hello, Regan."

He thought he felt her fingers tremble slightly before she pulled them from his grasp...but he couldn't be sure.

"I'd like you to meet Cal Benning," she said, turning to the man at her side. "Cal, this is Cody Fipes, Temptation's sheriff."

Regretfully, Cody turned to shake Cal's hand. "Pleased to meet you," he murmured, though he'd already decided to dislike the man on sight.

"A pleasure to meet you, too," Cal returned. He slung an arm around Regan's shoulders, smiling at Cody. "I've heard quite a bit about you from Reggie. According to her, you're the Lone Ranger and Wyatt Earp all rolled into one."

Cody narrowed his eyes at the familiarity the gesture suggested and the intimacy of this man using the name he'd always considered his own to use. He shifted his gaze to Regan's. Amber eyes, full of uncertainty, met his. "She's always had a tendency to stretch the truth a bit."

"Cody's just being modest," Mayor Acres interjected. "He keeps the law in this town, and I'm proud to say our crime rate is one of the lowest in the state."

"That's good to know," Cal replied, "since I'm

considering moving here." He turned to Reggie.
"Well, are we ready for the tour?"

Reggie lifted a shoulder. "Fine with me." She
turned to Cody. "Would you like to join us?"

The invitation seemed genuine enough, but Cody
quickly shook his head, sure that he couldn't stand
that kind of torture. Though spending the afternoon
with Regan held a certain appeal, having Cal Benning
along lessened the attraction. "No, y'all don't need
me. I've got some work to do."

He lifted his hat and rocked it back into place on
his head, then extended a hand to Cal...but only because it was expected of him. "Hope you find that
Temptation suits your needs." With a nod at Regan,
he turned and strode for the door.

Once outside, he paused, sucking in the first full
breath he'd drawn since entering Acres's office.

Across the street, Ruth Martin stood in front of the
Mercantile, a broom in one hand, frantically waving
with the other. On a sigh, Cody headed across the
street.

"Is that him?" she asked when he reached her,
tipping her head toward the mayor's office. "Is that
the man Regan's gonna sell the land to?"

Cody twisted his head around to stare at the may-
or's office door. "Yeah, that's him."

Ruth leaned on her broom handle and slowly
fanned her face. "My, but he's a looker, isn't he?
Haven't seen such a handsome face 'cept on the
movie screen. Kinda looks like a young Rock Hud-
son, don't you think?"

Cody frowned, his gaze still locked on the closed
door. "I really didn't pay much mind."

"Well, I certainly did. He seemed right friendly to Regan, too. Saw him offer her his arm like a real gentleman, then hold the door for her while she passed into the mayor's office ahead of him."

Cody stiffened, remembering seeing the same thing, but Ruth didn't seem to notice his discomfort, she just kept rattling on.

"Don't see much of that anymore. And he's young, too, did you notice? Probably about your age. Wonder if they've got something going? You never know these days. Why, they could be living together right now, for all we know. Young people are doing that more and more these—"

Cody whirled, his face tight with barely controlled fury. "Did you want something, Ruth? I need to get back to the office."

Ruth drew back as if offended. "Well, no. I just wanted to ask you if that was the man the town's all excited about." She gave her hand a wave, shooing Cody away. "Get on with your work. I'll just stand here a while and keep an eye on things."

Though he told himself he wasn't watching for her, Cody couldn't help noticing the shiny Lexus zip past his office several times that afternoon. He caught a glimpse of Regan behind the wheel, Cal on the passenger side and the mayor hanging over the front seat, his finger pointing out all that Temptation had to offer.

Cody shuffled papers on his desk, made the daily trek to the bank to oversee the pickup from the armored car, then headed straight back to his office.

He'd barely sat down behind his desk, when the

door opened. He glanced up as Mary Claire stuck her head through the opening.

"Hi, Cody. Am I interrupting anything?" she asked with a shy smile.

Cody shoved the paperwork aside and stood, grateful for the distraction. "Not a thing. Come on in." He crossed to the scarred table. "Can I buy you a cup of coffee?"

Mary Claire dropped down on one of the chairs in front of his desk with a sigh. "Sounds wonderful. I haven't had time for a cup since breakfast."

He poured them both a cup and set one in front of her before moving behind his desk and sitting again. "What brings you to town?" he asked.

She sipped, then sighed. "Last-minute shopping for the party tonight. You're coming, aren't you?"

Cody fished around in his head for an excuse, but nothing came to mind. "Not sure," he replied vaguely. "Got quite a bit of work to catch up on."

Mary Claire had a feeling that he might try to skip the festivities, which was exactly why she'd stopped by. She knew that something was brewing between Cody and Reggie, and thought they might need a little help. Hank and Leighanna had experienced a similar problem, and it was her scheming that had helped bring them together.

She pursed her lips in mock disappointment. "Oh, dear. And I was hoping I could ask you a favor."

"What?"

She waved his question away with a hand. "Nothing, really. I know you're busy. I suppose Harley could take care of it for me, though he does have his hands full at the house. He's barbecuing brisket for the party tonight, and you know how he is. It'll take a crowbar to pry him away from the grill. But that's not your problem.''

''Mary Claire, if you need me to do something, all you have to do is give the word.''

''Well,'' she replied hesitantly. ''With all the people, we're going to need extra ice. I brought several coolers with me. They're out in the van. I thought that if you were coming, you could fill them with ice at Ruth's store and bring them with you when you come. I'd take them with me now, but the ice would melt before tonight. But since you're not coming—''

Cody held up a hand, interrupting her. ''I'll bring the ice.'' He stood, setting his cup aside. ''I'll move the coolers from your van to my truck while you finish your coffee.''

As he walked past her, Mary Claire caught his hand. ''Thanks, Cody,'' she said, smiling up at him as she gave his hand a squeeze. ''You'll never know what a weight you've taken off my mind by agreeing to do this for me.''

The driveway was already crowded with cars and trucks when Cody arrived at the Kerr ranch. He wove his way through them, needing to get as close to the back of the house as possible so he could unload the coolers of ice.

He parked, then jumped out to lower the tailgate. From the corner of his eye, he saw Regan drive up with Cal as a passenger. They stepped from her Lexus laughing, and the sound sent a rod of steel up Cody's spine. Turning his back on them, he stretched and grabbed a handle, hauling a filled cooler to the edge of the truck's bed.

"Hey, Cody! Glad to see you again."

Stifling a groan, Cody turned to acknowledge the greeting.

"Cal," he replied, tipping his hat. He shifted his gaze to Regan. "Hello, Regan. How'd the day go?"

"Fine. Cal liked the Cooper place and is going to make an offer."

Cody shifted his gaze back to Cal, finding it easier to look at him than Regan. "That's good. I'm sure those folks will be more than happy to work out some kind of an agreement with you."

"I certainly hope so. I'm anxious to get my business relocated as soon as possible."

Unable to think of another thing to say to the two, Cody hefted the cooler. "If you'll excuse me, I promised Mary Claire I'd deliver the ice."

Cal quickly handed his briefcase to Regan. "Would you mind putting this inside for me? I'll help Cody with the coolers."

She took it, then, with a last glance at Cody, turned for the house.

"I can get 'em," Cody told Cal, shouldering him out of the way. "You might mess up your pretty clothes."

Cal bit back a smile. "Oh, I think I can manage." He caught the handle of a cooler and dragged it out. "Where are we going with these?" he asked pleasantly.

Already in motion, Cody gave his head a jerk in the direction of the patio where Mary Claire fussed over loaded tables. "I imagine she'll want them over there, close to the tables."

Walking side by side, the two men wove their way through the crowd of people filling the backyard.

"I understand that you and Reggie go way back," Cal said conversationally.

"Yeah," Cody muttered disagreeably. "Since we were kids."

"She's something, isn't she?" Cal chuckled. "Tried my damnedest to put a move on her the first time we met."

Cody jerked his head around to glare at Cal and found the man grinning at him.

"Don't worry," Cal reassured him. "She let me know real quick that she wasn't interested in a relationship." He turned his head to look at Regan's retreating back. "I figured there must be someone else in the picture, though she denied it. But I can see now that I was right."

Cody stopped, balancing the cooler on a knee, while he grabbed at Cal's arm, stopping him, too. "What are you getting at?"

Cal turned to face Cody, looking at him in surprise. "Are you blind? The woman's never had eyes for anyone else because she's always been in love with you."

Though he had planned to deliver the ice then head back to town, Cody ended up staying for the party. Why, he wasn't sure, because it was pure torture to be near Regan when he knew damn good and well that she'd be leaving again the next day.

...and she's always been in love with you.

Cody shook his head, trying to jar Cal's words from his mind. He knew Regan loved him, she'd told him so often enough. And he loved her. But he was also wise enough to know that sometimes love simply wasn't enough.

"Okay, everybody gather around," Harley called out as he stepped through the kitchen door, carrying a cake. Cody shifted to the fringe of the crowd that immediately gathered around Regan.

Unaware that the party had been planned in her honor, she pressed her hands to her cheeks. "Oh, Harley," she cried.

"Happy birthday, little sister," he said, grinning. He nodded toward the chair at the head of the table. "Take a seat while I get this forest fire set to burn."

Everyone moved to circle the table while Harley set the birthday cake in front of Regan—everyone except Cody. He hung back on the edge, waiting for her to cut the cake so he could make a quick exit without drawing attention to his departure.

Harley chuckled as he struck a match and began lighting candles. "I remember the last birthday party I planned for you," he said, with a rueful shake of his head. "It was your eighteenth birthday." He blew out the match, then slung an arm around Cody's shoulder, drawing him to his side. "And Cody here was the only one who showed up."

Regan twisted around to stare at Cody, her eyes growing round. "You came back?" she murmured, her gaze locked on his.

Red-cheeked, Cody ducked his head. "Yeah, but I was too late. You were already gone."

Slowly, Reggie rose. "But you came," she insisted, moving toward him. "I never knew."

Cody's mouth curled in a scowl. "How could you?" he asked bitterly. "You left without bothering to tell anyone where you were headed." Feeling the curious gaze of all the guests, he quickly retrieved his hat and nodded his head toward Harley and Mary Claire. "I guess I better be going. Thanks for the invite."

Her heart in her throat, Reggie watched him leave.

"What was that all about?" Mary Claire asked in confusion.

Reggie heaved an angry breath. "I'm not sure, but I'm damn sure going to find out. He ruined one birthday for me. He's not going to ruin another."

Reggie opened the door to Cody's office then slammed it shut behind her. Cody didn't even glance up.

Marching across the room to his desk, she stopped, folding her arms angrily beneath her breasts. "Why did you leave?" she asked, her voice tight with carefully suppressed anger.

Cody kept his gaze on the papers on his desk. "I had work to do."

"No, I mean then, eleven years ago."

Dragging a weary hand down his face, Cody looked up at her. "What do you want, Regan?"

"I want an explanation."

He stared at her a moment, his gray eyes as unrelenting as steel. "Well, you're not getting one."

He picked up his pen again and Reggie yanked it from his hand. "You *owe* me an explanation," she said, throwing the pen hard against the far wall. "And I intend to hear it."

He rocketed from his chair, planting his hands on his desk as he glared at her. "I owe *you* an explanation? I'd think you owe *me* one."

"For what!" Reggie cried.

"You're the one who left, hauling butt for the big city, not telling anyone where you were going."

"But you left first! That's why I ran away. With you gone, there wasn't any reason to stay. You broke my heart when you left Temptation. And you broke it again three weeks ago when you let me return to Houston when you knew damn good and well that I wanted to stay right here in Temptation with you."

A flicker of hope sparked in Cody's eyes, then quickly died. "It's no good, Regan," he said wearily as he dropped back down in his chair. "It would never work for us."

She fisted her hands on her hips. "And why not?"

"Because you're a wealthy woman with a wealthy woman's taste. I'm nothing but a two-bit sheriff in a small town that can barely afford to pay my salary."

Reggie stared at him, her eyes filling with tears, crushed that he'd think so little of her. "You know what, Cody? I've been supporting myself since I was eighteen and doing a damn good job of it, I might add. But I never wanted the money or what it bought me. All I ever wanted was you."

Before he could respond, she spun and marched for the door, slamming it behind her. Wanted posters flapped in the breeze she created.

"Damn it all to hell," Cody muttered and shoved the papers from his desk.

* * *

The next morning, Cody was in his office early. He'd had a long sleepless night to think over his decision, and though he still wasn't sure he was doing the right thing, he was doing it.

Box in hand, he glanced up to see Harley standing in the open office door, watching him. Frowning, Cody stuffed a fistful of file folders into the box and reached for another.

"Going somewhere?" Harley asked lazily as he closed the door behind him.

"Yeah." Cody yanked off his badge and threw it onto the desk. "I'm leaving Temptation."

Harley dropped down on one of the chairs in front of Cody's desk and hooked his hat over his knee, shaking his head. "I never knew you to be a coward before, Cody."

Cody lifted his chin, narrowing his eyes at Harley. "Sometimes it takes more guts to leave than to stay."

Harley reared back in the chair, tipping it on two legs. "Where're you headed?"

"Houston. I figure a man would have a better opportunity for making a living there than here." What he didn't say, was that in Houston, he'd be near Regan.

Harley neither agreed or disagreed with Cody's statement. He simply nodded his head in the direction of the window. "Funny, isn't it? You're moving to Houston and Regan's moving to Temptation. She's over at Ruth's right now, trying to talk her into leasing her that vacant building beside her store."

Cody jerked his head toward the window and sure enough there was Regan's Lexus, parked in front of the Mercantile. "What does she need an office for?"

Harley chuckled, shaking his head. "She's planning to open a real estate office here in Temptation. What with the town growing like it is, she feels there'll be a need for an honest realtor before long." He ducked his head, then lifted it, leveling an eye at Cody. "I know what's between you two. Have, since we were all nothing but kids. You were right to leave before. Regan was too young to know her own mind. But she's mature now, and more than capable of making her own decisions. You might give leaving again some thought."

Having had his say, Harley dropped the chair to all four legs and rose. "But I wouldn't take too long thinking about it," he warned. "Sister or not, the woman's got a temper that only gets worse with time."

Nine

Cody stared at the window long after Harley had left, still unable to believe that Regan would leave Houston and all that she'd worked for there to move back to Temptation.

If what Harley had said was correct, then that meant that everything Regan had said to him the night before was true, as well. The money and all the things it bought meant nothing to her.

He picked up his badge, palming it a moment before pinning it back on his pocket. He prayed she meant the other part, too, the part where she'd said that all she'd ever wanted was him.

Yanking open a drawer, he pulled out a pad, then slammed the drawer closed with his knee. Hauling in a deep breath he headed across the street. He stopped beside Regan's Lexus, flipped open the pad and began to write.

* * *

Reggie extended her hand. "Thanks, Ruth. I'll draw up a contract for us to sign and drop it by later this afternoon."

Ruth shook Reggie's hand then dropped it. "Pshaw. We don't need no contract. Your handshake on the deal is good enough for me."

Reggie bit back a smile. Some things in Temptation would never change. A man's word—or a woman's, it seemed—was all that was needed to seal an agreement.

Catching a movement out of the corner of her eye, she turned toward the store's plate glass window. Cody stood on the street beside her car, scribbling something on a pad.

"What in the world is he doing?" she murmured, her eyes widening.

Ruth cackled. "Looks to me like he's writing you a ticket."

Reggie's mouth dropped open. Outraged, she stormed out of the Mercantile and out onto the walk. "What do you think you're doing?" she cried indignantly.

"Writing you a ticket."

"A ticket!"

Cody glanced up at her and frowned, then dropped his gaze back to his pad. "Yes, ma'am. You're illegally parked in a loading zone."

"That's ridiculous! You know as well as I do that everyone ignores that sign."

"What everyone else does, doesn't interest me. The fact of the matter is, you're parked illegally in an area clearly marked as a loading zone."

All the anger, all the frustration from the night be-

fore, came humming back to sting. Reggie reared
back and took a swing at him, but Cody quickly
grabbed her wrist and twisted it behind her back. Before Reggie could even draw a shocked breath, he had
a pair of handcuffs slapped around her wrists.

"You're under arrest."

Reggie twisted her head around to gawk at him
over her shoulder. "For what?" she demanded to
know.

"Assaulting an officer of the law."

Reggie lifted her foot and kicked hard behind her.
Cody sidestepped, dodging the blow. "And for resisting arrest," he added dryly. Taking her elbow, he
guided her kicking and screaming across the street,
into his office, then on to the cell at the rear.

Once inside, Reggie wheeled on him. "Cody, this
is ridiculous. Take these handcuffs off me right this
instant."

In answer, Cody pulled the cell door closed behind
him, locking them both inside. "Can't just yet. I need
to read you your rights first."

Her amber eyes flamed as she inhaled a sharp
breath. "Cody Fipes, I'm warning you..."

Slowly, he turned to face her. "Are you threatening
an officer of the law?"

The menacing quirk of his brow, the look of smug
pleasure on his face angered Reggie all the more. She
didn't know what he hoped to prove by throwing
around his weight as sheriff and she didn't intend to
stick around long enough to find out. "I'll pay your
stupid fine," she grated out. "Just tell me how much
it is."

Cody leaned back, propping a boot against a bar

on the cell door, and folded his arms beneath the star on his chest. He pursed his lips thoughtfully. "Well, let's see. There's the parking violation, that'll run you thirty-five dollars. Then there's the charge of resisting arrest which'll cost you another hundred and fifty.

"Of course, we can't forget the assault on an officer," he added. "Temptation doesn't look kindly on those who rough up their sheriff. That one's gonna cost you a minimum of five hundred." He twisted his mouth, touching three fingers in turn to the ball of his thumb as he totaled it all up. "Thirty-five plus a hundred and fifty is one-eighty-five. Plus the five hundred brings your total to a whopping six hundred and eighty-five dollars."

Reggie sucked in a furious breath. "I'll pay."

Cody just looked at her, his expression never once wavering. "With what?"

She cast about, looking for her purse, then remembered that she'd left it on the counter at Ruth's store. "I'll need to go over to the Mercantile and get my purse." She twisted around, thrusting her handcuffed wrists to him. "If you'll get these things off me, I'll get my checkbook and pay your ridiculous fine."

"Checkbook?" Cody repeated. "Sorry. We only accept cash."

Reggie dropped her chin to her chest in frustration. "I don't carry that much cash," she mumbled miserably.

"Smart woman. Nobody should carry that much money around. Just asking for trouble, if they do."

Slowly Reggie turned. "Then what do you suggest I do?"

Cody lifted a shoulder. "I suppose I could call you

a bail bondsman, though it would probably take him a couple of hours to get here."

Reggie's chin snapped up at the reminder. "I'm entitled to a phone call. I'll call Harley. He'll pay my fine."

Cody pushed off the bars, bracing his feet wide as he slipped his fingers beneath his belt to tuck his shirt in more neatly. "You could, but you probably wouldn't find him. He'd be out on the ranch by now."

"Mary Claire, then. She'll come."

"I'm sure she would…if she were home," he added. "She was to meet Hank and Leighanna over at her old house this morning. Seems that Hank and Leighanna are wanting to lease the place from her. What with the baby coming and all, they'll be needing the room. You could try calling there, but if memory serves me right, Mary Claire had the phone disconnected when she moved in with Harley."

Reggie bit back a moan. She knew that Mary Claire was meeting Hank and Leighanna. She was even supposed to meet them there later and help draw up the lease. Frustrated, she sank down on the sagging cot, her hands hanging limply at her back.

She looked so pitiful sitting there, Cody wondered if maybe he hadn't carried this all a bit too far. "Harley tells me you're moving to Temptation to open up a real estate office."

She jerked her head up to look at him, firming her lips. "Yes, I am."

He nodded sagely in that slow way of his. "Kind of a big step down financially, isn't it?"

She lifted her chin imperiously. "I never take on something without weighing the consequences first."

Cody wondered about her declaration of love so many years before and wondered if she'd weighed that, as well, before approaching him to run away with her. Though Harley had said she was too young then to know her mind, Cody disagreed. Regan had always known what she wanted, even when they were kids, and never hesitated in her pursuit of whatever goal she set her heart and mind on. He was only beginning to realize that she'd meant what she'd said about loving him, both then and now.

He folded his arms across his chest. The star on his pocket caught the sun streaming through the small window above her head and shot a spot of light on the opposite wall. "Would you consider taking on a partner?"

Stunned, she stared. "A partner?" she repeated dully.

"Yeah. A partner." He took a step toward her and unfolded his arms. "I've got the money, if that concerns you." He hunkered down in front of her and lifted a hand to smooth the pad of his thumb across her cheek. "Set it back quite a few years ago when I was riding the rodeo circuit. Had hoped to use the money to buy us a place of our own when you turned eighteen."

Tears sprinted to Reggie's eyes. "Us?" she whispered, sure that she had misunderstood him.

"Yeah, us."

Curling her hands into fists within the handcuffs, Reggie leaned back, pulling away from his touch, not at all sure what all this meant. "Is this a marriage proposal you're offering or a business deal?"

A self-conscious grin chipped at Cody's mouth. "A

little of both, I guess. After all, a man's got his pride." He leaned closer, until his lips were inches away from her face. "I love you, Regan. I'm in love with you, and have been for as long as I can remember. If you'll give me a chance, I'd like to prove just how much."

Her hands trembling within the handcuffs, Reggie blinked back tears. "Get these things off me."

Not sure what kind of answer that was, Cody stood, catching her elbow and drawing her up with him. She turned, thrusting her cuffed wrists to him. Cody drew the ring of keys from his pocket, inserted the key. "Now you're not going to start swinging at me again, are you?"

Reggie dropped her head back to keep from screaming. "No."

"Or kick or claw at my face?"

Reggie braced her arms and lifted them higher behind her. "For God's sake, Cody, just get the cuffs off!" she cried.

On a sigh, he turned the lock and the cuffs slipped free, falling to hit the floor at her feet. But before she could move, he caught her wrist and slowly turned her, bringing her hand to his mouth. With his gaze on hers, he pressed his lips against the red mark the cuffs had left on her wrist and felt a thrill of relief when he felt her pulse quicken, saw the heat that flamed in her eyes. "I love you, Reggie," he murmured softly. "I want you to marry me and be my wife."

Pulling free, Reggie threw her arms around his neck. "Oh, Cody," she cried.

He chuckled, squeezing her hard against him. "Is that a yes?"

She grabbed his cheeks between her hands. "Of course it's a yes!" she cried, laughing. "I've waited eleven years for this and was scared to death I was going to have to do the asking again."

He caught her to him, hugging her tight against his chest. "I'm sorry, Reggie, for all the lost years."

She flattened her hands against his chest, pushing far enough away so that she could look at him. "I'm not," she whispered. "You were always with me in my heart."

She couldn't have said anything that would've pleased Cody more. He caught her hand. "Come on. I've got to ask Harley for your hand and make this official."

At the door to the cell, he stopped. "Uh-oh," he murmured, his face turning a bright red.

Reggie looked up at him in concern. "What's wrong?"

"It seems we have a little problem here," he murmured, staring at the lock.

"What?" she asked and followed the line of his gaze.

"The door's locked."

Reggie laughed, wrapping an arm around his waist and hugging him to her. "Well, unlock it, silly."

Cody turned to her, wearing a sheepish grin. "That's the problem. The key's on my desk."

Reggie's eyes widened. "You mean we're locked in here?"

"Sure looks that way."

"But how will we get out?"

He lifted a shoulder in that lazy way that Reggie found so endearing. "Somebody'll come along before long. Until they do..." He stooped and caught her beneath the knees, lifting her into his arms. "I guess we'll just have to make do."

With a glance at the bare, sagging cot behind her, Reggie laced her hands around his neck. "Yeah, I guess we will."

Epilogue

Cody stood on the deck, his back braced against its rail, staring back at the two-story log cabin he and Reggie had built on the site of the cabin he'd grown up in. Though he'd been against it at first, it hadn't taken Reggie long to convince him that they should build their home there. Mary Claire and Harley were within shouting distance, she'd told him, and Hank and Leighanna were just a short drive away down the road. In the end, he'd knuckled under, as everyone knew he would. Seemed he was destined to be a fool for anything Reggie wanted.

He'd even accepted sharing his private name for her with the world. It made him proud to know that she'd chosen it, even when they were apart.

The late afternoon sun turned the windows to gold while he stared, and the smell of freshly cut cedar mingled with the scent of mesquite burning in the stone barbecue pit he'd built with his own hands. Through the open French doors drifted the sound of Reggie's soft humming.

Three-sixty, he thought with a sigh. He'd done a smooth three-sixty. Living here as a kid, then returning as a married man to make his home on the land Buster Fipes had left him. He chuckled, turning around to brace his hands on the hand-hewn rail and staring out at the five acres he'd cleared and fenced with Harley and Hank's help. If anyone had ever suggested to him that he'd be making his home here, he'd have told them they were crazy. Even when he'd lived here before, the place had never been home.

But Reggie made the difference.

His shoulders lifted and fell on a satisfied sigh. No matter where they lived, he knew that as long as he was with Reggie, he would be home.

A lot of things had changed for him over the last year. He'd become a husband, a father, even added on a new career. He shook his head, still amazed that Reggie had talked him into buying a tract of land and building houses on it. Him, a builder. Who'd have ever thought it?

But he'd taken on the challenge, balancing his duties as sheriff with the responsibilities of supervising subcontractors. All in all, he was pretty pleased with the way things had turned out.

"Cody?"

He cocked his head to look over his shoulder. "Out here, honey."

Reggie stepped through the open French doors, balancing the baby on her hip. Cody's heart turned over at the sight of the woman he loved and the son they'd created together. Crossing to meet them, he dropped a kiss on Reggie's cheek and held out his arms. "Come here, cowboy, and let your daddy have a look at you." Taking his son from Reggie, he dropped his hat on the baby's head and lifted him high in the air. Chortling, the infant grabbed the side flaps of the hat and pulled them over his ears.

"He's going to ruin your hat," Reggie warned.

"So I'll buy another one."

Reggie folded her arms beneath her breasts and sighed. "You're going to spoil him."

Cody glanced at her and grinned as he settled his son on his hip. "That's what babies are for, aren't they?" he asked as he drew Reggie to his other side.

She tipped her face up to his, her love for her husband shining in her amber eyes. "Wives, too?"

He lowered his face to hers. "Yeah, wives, too," he murmured before pressing his lips to hers.

"Kissy. Kissy. Kissy," Stephie called in a sing-songy voice.

Cody grinned against Reggie's lips. "I believe the troops have arrived."

He turned, draping an arm around Reggie to see the Kerrs trudging their way around the house. Stephie led the way, skipping, followed by Jimmy who struggled beneath the weight of a cooler. Leigh-anna, cuddling a curly-headed infant, brought up the rear.

"Sorry we're late," Mary Claire called out breathlessly as she climbed the steps to the deck. Seven months pregnant, she already waddled like a duck. Her face broke into a smile when Cody, Jr. reached for her. "Aren't you precious," she cooed, stealing him away from his daddy. "You know who loves you the most, don't you, darling?"

Cody planted his hands on his hips, frowning. "He only wants you because you feed him chocolate."

Mary Claire lifted her head and grinned wickedly. "Whatever works." She shooed Cody away with a wave of her hand when he reached to reclaim his son. "Go do something useful, like help Hank with the keg. We've got a party to throw, remember? Cal and his people will be arriving any minute."

Scowling, Cody shot his traitorous son one last look, knowing he probably wouldn't see him again until everybody was gone. On a sigh, he loped down the steps, meeting Harley and Hank who carried the keg between them.

"Beer's here!" Hank called out, grinning. "Where's the food?"

"Brisket's on the grill, smoking." Cody glanced up at the sound of a horn. A line of cars slowly made their way down the winding drive. Cal Benning's Jaguar led the parade.

While Hank and Harley carried the keg onto the deck, Cody stopped, bracing his hands on his hips, his chest swelling with pride as he watched the line of cars draw near.

Between them, he and Reggie had done what no one had thought possible. They'd saved Temptation from becoming a ghost town.

Reggie slipped up behind him, wrapping her arms at his waist. "Penny for your thoughts," she whispered before pressing her lips against his back.

Cody turned, tucking her under his arm. "They're worth a helluva lot more than that."

Lifting her face to his, Reggie smiled as she hugged him to her. "Pretty proud of yourself, aren't you?"

"Proud of *us*," he corrected. "Come on," he said, pulling her along with him. "Let's go greet Temptation's newest residents."

* * * * *

They called her the

Champagne Girl

Catherine: Underneath the effervescent, carefree and bubbly facade there was a depth to which few had access.

Matt: The older stepbrother she inherited with her mother's second marriage, Matt continually complicated things. It seemed to Catherine that she would make plans only to have Matt foul them up.

With the perfect job waiting in New York City, only one thing would be able to keep her on a dusty cattle ranch: something she thought she could never have—the love of the sexiest cowboy in the Lone Star state.

by bestselling author

DIANA PALMER

Available in September 1997 at your favorite retail outlet.

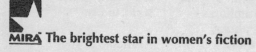

MIRA The brightest star in women's fiction

MDP8

Look us up on-line at: http://www.romance.net

SILHOUETTE® *Desire*®

15 YEARS OF GUARANTEED GOOD READING!

Desire has always brought you satisfying novels that let you escape into a world of endless possibilities— with heroines who are in control of their lives and heroes who bring them passionate romance beyond their wildest dreams.

When you pick up a Silhouette Desire, you can be confident that you won't be disappointed. Desire always has six fresh and exciting titles every month by your favorite authors— **Diana Palmer, Ann Major, Dixie Browning, Lass Small and BJ James,** just to name a few. Watch for extraspecial stories by these and other authors in **October, November and December 1997** as we celebrate **Desire's 15th anniversary.**

Indulge yourself with three months of top authors and fabulous reading…we even have a fantastic promotion waiting for you!

Pick up a Silhouette Desire… it's what women want today.

Available at your favorite retail outlet.

FANTASTIC NEWS!

For all you devoted Diana Palmer fans
Silhouette Books is pleased to bring you
a brand-new novel and short story by one of the
top ten romance writers in America

"Nobody tops Diana Palmer...I love her stories."
—New York Times **bestselling author
Jayne Ann Krentz**

**Diana Palmer has written another thrilling desire.
Man of the Month Ramon Cortero was a talented
surgeon, existing only for his work—until the
night he saved nurse Noreen Kensington's life. But
their stormy past makes this romance a challenge!**

THE PATIENT NURSE
Silhouette Desire
October 1997

And in November Diana Palmer adds to the
Long, Tall Texans series with *CHRISTMAS COWBOY*, in
LONE STAR CHRISTMAS, a fabulous new holiday
keepsake collection by talented authors Diana Palmer
and Joan Johnston. Their heroes are seductive,
shameless and irresistible—and these Texans are
experts at sneaking kisses under the mistletoe! So get
ready for a sizzling holiday season....

Only from

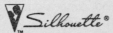